vol 1, issue 2

EDITED BY
RICK OLLERMAN

Down & Out Books
3959 Van Dyke Road, Suite 265
Lutz, FL 33558
DownAndOutBooks.com

The characters and events in this book are fictitious. Any similarity to real persons, living or dead, is coincidental and not intended by the author.

Cover photo © by Peter Rozovsky
Cover design by Lance Wright

ISBN: 1-946502-85-5
ISBN-13: 978-1-946502-85-8

CONTENTS

A Few Clues from the Editor
Rick Ollerman

Welcome back, everybody. And if you're a new reader for our second issue, thanks for giving us a look. We're a bit delayed as we've found that I've proven to be less than indestructible this summer following a broken wrist (a skateboard, a thirteen-year-old son, and a bit of bad judgment; he puts his feet on the front of his board and keeps going, I try the same and go backwards—who knew?) and some more knee surgery because at this point, why not? The main thing is that after a collection of braces and casts I'm finally able to type again, and therefore edit and write and do all the things I was supposed to be doing all along. Fortunately I can apologize to various publishers over the phone, whether they want to hear it or not.

The first issue was a big success, which was wonderful. We take that to mean that everything we tried to do was what people were looking for in a new crime fiction magazine. The trick of course is to keep it going. This issue we bring you stories that I think are every bit as strong as those in the first, including a new Sheriff Dan Rhodes story from the redoubtable Bill Crider.

The best news may be that by the time you read this, the subscription program will finally be up and running. Not only does this ensure you'll receive each issue in a sturdy non-bubble-wrappy mailer but a series of coupons that will more than pay for the subscription itself should you choose to use them. The choice is an easy one. Subscribe today. Tell your mom.

Most of the feedback I've received about the magazine has been through word of mouth at conferences like Bouchercon and some through personal emails, but if you're moved to go more in depth, by all means online reviews can only help garner more readers—always

1

the goal, we are a magazine—but also feel free to send feedback to rick@downandoutmagazine.com. We would love to hear from you.

So from time to time I come up with topics that I use to focus discussions around when I go to conferences or speak at various events. Lately I've been noodling around with the notion that with only the five big publishing companies in New York (the "Big Five"), and the fact that forty years ago there were dozens, is in fact hurting the quality of the crime fiction we see today. That's the argument and I illustrate it by saying I truly believe if you were to stick your hand in a big box of paperback original era Fawcett Gold Medal paperbacks and pick one at random, you are much likely to pick up a book that is more suspenseful, more original, has fewer plot holes, and has stronger characters than if you were to do the same thing with a random boxful of Big Five crime thrillers.

I think this is because New York's thinking isn't "give me a great new book" it's "give me another book like last year's and the year before's," or if you're Joe Smith, "Give me this year's Joe Smith book." They don't read it the same way, they don't edit it the same way: it's the name on the cover that's already sold it.

The "Hollywood blockbuster" mentality doesn't help either, where if Marketing doesn't feel a title won't sell x number of titles they're just not going to take a chance on it. Publishing didn't put these restrictions on themselves back in the fifties and sixties. Don't get me wrong, there were plenty of clunkers back then too, there always have been, I'm just postulating not as many as we have now.

Those are my fighting words. What do you think? As a past judge of a major award I can tell you just how hard it is to come up with enough contemporary books to even fill the nominations, let alone find one to even feel good enough about to name the winner. In many ways the Big Five era vs. the PBO era seems to be one of "good enough" vs. originality.

Okay. Light me up. My email is rick@downandoutmagazine.com. Be gentle. I'm injured.

Lissa (pronounced "Lisa") Marie Redmond is a retired cold case and homicide detective from Buffalo, now turned writer. Actually, now turned very, very good writer. Her first novel in a projected trilogy will be released in February 2018 by Midnight Ink called A Cold Day in Hell. *One of her short stories was a standout in Akashic's* Buffalo Noir *(2015) and this one,* One at a Time, *is another...*

One at a Time
Lissa Marie Redmond

It's just my luck to get locked in a trunk of a car so old there's no emergency latch. I pulled every wire, but it's so late and the roads so desolate the chances of getting pulled over for a tail light infraction are pretty slim. The original tire jack is long gone, along with the spare. I can feel the wheel turning close to my head and scooch forward as far as I can. The shocks on this Ford are shot, my head keeps smashing into the trunk lid with every bump. I'll probably die of a concussion before they get a chance to kill me another way.

I messed up. But then again, I've always been a screw-up. Victor knew that when he hired me. Now I'm about to be driven out to the woods somewhere in a broken down 1969 Ford Fairlane that's older than me to get my brains blown out.

It smells like rust and exhaust fumes, it's choking me, making my eyes water. I run my hand across what's left of the carpeting back here. The corner feels squishy; damp and sticky. Blood.

I'm not the first person to take this ride.

Jacki got me into this. Jacki with an "i." She came up to me at McGruder's Bar in South Buffalo a week ago and said she had a sure-fire job for me. Jacki had been bartending there for a couple of years and I was one of her steady customers when I wasn't locked up. She always managed to get a tip out of me, mainly because of

3

the tight shirts she liked to wear but also because she was nice to me when she didn't have to be. She knew I'd just got out of the county jail. She knew I was always strapped for cash because I was drinking shitty draft beer. She knew I'd take one look at that short skirt and say yes.

"Let's go for a ride, Marcus," she said, putting her half empty bottle on the bar.

I finished my draft with a giant gulp, beer dribbling down my chin onto my ratty Sabres jersey. "Where we going?"

"Victor wants me to show you something."

Victor never got his own hands dirty. He'd always been too smart for that. So I followed Jacki out to her brand new black BMW and tried not to get any of the grease that was embedded in my clothes and hands on the smooth leather of the upholstery.

"I heard Joe Marella has you cleaning up his body shop these days," she said, dropping the car in gear.

"He owed me, from my last job," I said, trying not to watch her skirt ride up her thighs as she manipulated the gas and brake.

Her black curls fell around her face as she nodded. "He's a good guy."

She drove west, toward the water. The sun had already sunk down into Lake Erie and a starless night hung overhead. Jacki hummed as she drove. Someone told me she wanted to be a singer once, before she met Victor. Victor had a way of altering your trajectory. I'm living proof of that. For the moment anyway.

She pulled into the parking lot of one of Buffalo's numerous derelict grain elevators. It was a crumbling, broken down wreck, not one of the fashionable "artsy" ones the preservationists had poetry readings at down by Canalside. Hundreds of men had once parked for work there every day but now it was a dumping ground. Ripped, overflowing olive-green garbage bags littered the cracked asphalt. A burned-out shell of a car was propped against one of the buildings, black scorch marks rising up from the skeleton. The only illumination came from the street lights that lined Ohio Street, casting a dim glow over the section of the lot where Jacki parked us.

She sat there looking at me until I asked, "What am I supposed to see?"

"In exactly seven days Victor needs you to bring something to this spot. This spot right here. Not the handicap spot two over, or over by that chain link fence. Right. Fucking. Here."

I nodded. "Okay. I get it. What exactly am I supposed to deliver?"

She arched an eyebrow at me. "Really?"

I shrugged. "Am I buying something? Selling something? Hurting something? What?"

"You're going to park a car right here, leave the keys in the ignition, and walk away."

"That's it?"

"That's it." She licked the cherry red lip gloss on her bottom lip. I tried to focus.

"How much for me?"

"Victor's feeling generous. Ten grand. No questions asked."

Ten grand. I could do a lot with ten grand. Buy myself a decent car and go to my sister's in Florida. Her boyfriend could find me something to do. He was good like that. At twenty-nine years old, I'd spent a total of four years of my life in and out of prison. Ten grand could get me the hell out of Buffalo. Away from the grain elevators, away from the mountains of snow and away from scrubbing out Joey Marella's toilets for twelve bucks an hour off the books. Ten grand could buy me a life.

I shook my head. "Too good to be true."

"The envelope will be in the glove box. Pick it up from point A, you drive it to point B. No stops. You walk away and you take the money with you. What could be easier?"

"It's never easy with you, Jacki."

She leaned over and whispered in my ear, "Ten grand can buy you a lot of easy, Marcus. It's a yes or no proposition. Victor needs an answer right now."

I said yes, of course.

In the end, it always comes down to greed, doesn't it? I've thought about this for the last week and I should've been happy, driving a rattle trap car to a vacant grain mill for ten grand, but what if I could somehow make it eleven grand? Or fifteen grand? Or a hundred grand? That's the way my mind works, it always has. If this is a good angle, there has to be a better one. The problem is I'm no good at geometry. That's why I end up in jail so much. And why Victor's guy is going to put a bullet into my skull as soon as we get wherever we're going.

This car groans and creaks like my grandmother's knees. The suspension is shot and the rattling muffler could fall off with the next bump in the pavement. It's a throwaway, like me. Over a hundred thousand hard miles on it and still counting. Taken from a junk yard somewhere where it probably should have been left to die at the end of a hard life. No one will miss it, just like no one will miss me.

I feel around the interior again. My cellphone is dead, so I have no light. There's no spare, no tire iron, no fix-a-flat. When this old ass antique of a vehicle stops, I'm going to be dead.

I started out okay. Jacki gave me a nail salon flyer with the address of where to pick up the car and the time when it would be there. I had Joey Marella drop me there after work. The rusty red Ford Fairlane was parked in front of what used to be an old bakery on Warsaw Avenue. I knew Victor owned the building and leased the upstairs apartment to some of his working girls but it was early in the day and no one would be around. I waved Joey off—who thought I was going to pay one of the girls a visit, then I walked up one side of the street and back down the other until I thought I was alone and good to approach the car.

The keys were dangling from the ignition lock along with a fuzzy green shamrock. That should have been my first warning but I was too worried about getting out of there to think about it. One of the leaves had broken off the key chain, making it a two-leaf clover. Second warning? Bad luck, anyway.

The door wasn't locked and I sank down into the spongy front bench seat. The car was the size of a battleship. I tried the heater. Of course it didn't work. Why would you want a working heater in Buffalo in February?

Putting the Ford in reverse, I backed out of the space and then started heading for the grain elevator. It was icy out and the tires were bald, so I kept slipping and sliding. With every stop I was hearing something heavy thumping and bumping around. The more I heard it, the more I wanted to see what it was.

What could be the harm in unlocking the trunk?

I was too stupid to answer my own question.

Victor said don't look, just drive. But how would Victor know if I took a peek? Just a look see, for my own curiosity, you know? What Victor didn't know I knew wouldn't hurt me right?

The problem was: Victor always knows. That's why he's the boss.

I heard the thump again as I turned into the empty elevator lot. Instead of pulling into the designated spot as directed, I pulled into a little alley between two small abandoned buildings. The windows were long smashed out, leaving sharp little glass teeth in the otherwise empty panes. Snow was tumbling down in big, fat flakes between the red brick walls. I looked up at the sliver of sky showing and saw dirty gray clouds. It was late afternoon, but it might just as well have been twilight. I rubbed my gloved hands together against the bitter cold and unlocked the trunk. The whole place stunk like Cheerios, like they make in the factories here. The falling snow could have been frozen drops of milk.

Inside the trunk, bound with duct tape, was Joey Marella's nineteen-year-old son. I had heard rumors that Justin had a big mouth, running around selling pills and hiding behind his father's repuretion. But I also heard he got busted two weeks ago holding two ounces of coke and a shiny new FMK 9mm. Him being duct taped hand and foot, with another piece wrapped around his entire head, mouth included, likely meant just one thing: he had rolled on Victor. He meant for him to freeze to death in the trunk, which Joey would recognize as a harsh message to keep the rest of his people in line. The word would get out and I would get the blame. No ten grand for me, just a one-way ticket back to Attica.

Justin was trying to talk, or at least make a noise. They had worked him over pretty good. He had two black eyes and his nose was crooked. I reached down with both hands and tried to tear the layers of tape covering his mouth but it was too slick with his saliva and snot. I had to dig at an end and unwrap the tape from his head, pulling the hair from the back of his head. "Marcus, please," he begged. But with his new lack of teeth it came out more like *pleethzz.* "Help me, Marcus. Don't let them do this."

I'd known Justin since he was just a skinny kid hanging around his dad's shop. He'd come in with his toy cars and pretend to fix them with the plastic tool kit he'd got on his birthday. He knew how to make coffee when he was eight, knew where we stashed the vintage *Playboys* by ten and knew which guy liked what beer by the time he was twelve.

I looked down at him wriggling around in the trunk. "Did you tell the police about Victor?"

"I had to, man! They said I was looking at twenty years. The detective told me no one would ever know."

"They lied."

"Just let me go. I'll disappear. I swear, you'll never see me again..."

Joey Marella and his wife had me over for Christmas dinner, maybe six years ago. I don't have a family anymore: my dad died in jail and my mom lit out when I was thirteen and left me with my dad's brother. I always thought Joey felt sorry for me because he was all about family. Especially his mother, who always sat at the head of the dining room table like she was the Queen of England. That Christmas I was perched on the edge of one of the extra metal chairs they had pulled up to make room for me. I stuffed so much ham and potatoes in my mouth I thought I'd explode, my stomach bulging over my jeans.

Joey's mom kept shoveling food on my plate. "You're too skinny!" she said in her thick Sicilian accent. All around, Joey's nieces and nephews were chasing each other in circles, making a loud racket but nobody minded. When it came time to open the presents we moved our chairs into the living room. Joey's wife, Connie, handed out the gifts and we watched the kids rip through the wrapping paper, tearing at the boxes inside.

I was drinking a whiskey sour because everyone drank whiskey sours at Joey's house on Christmas, when Justin came up to me. He had a box topped with a big blue bow and was offering it to me.

"What's this?" I'd asked him.

"It's for you," he said. He was thirteen years old then, his voice breaking, face dusted with acne.

I took the box. "Why'd you get me a present?"

He stood waiting. "Just open it."

I knew his mom had wrapped it for him: the kid couldn't tie a bow to save his life. So I tore into the paper that had miniature candy canes on it and opened the box. A brand new crescent wrench sat nestled in a crumpled wad of white tissue paper.

"What's this for? I didn't get you anything."

He shrugged. "You don't have any of your own tools. You always borrow my dad's and he says everyone needs to build their own collection one piece at a time. Now," he said, embarrassed, "you have your first piece."

I wanted to hug him, kind of, or pat him on the back, or do something, but I'm not the kind of guy who knows what to do when someone gives you something and doesn't want anything back for it. I was young myself, twenty-three or twenty-four, and just out of jail again. I got a lump in my throat as I took that wrench out of its box. "Thanks, Justin. It's a great present."

And it was.

I pulled out my pocket knife and sawed at the duct tape at his ankles. "Listen to me. Victor will find you. You need to go back to the cops, right now. Tell them about this. I have to park the car so everything seems legit. You have to go all in, tell them everything." You could see the car from Ohio Street. Victor would send someone to cruise by to make sure I'd done what he asked. He was thorough like that. Having it sit there would buy us some time. Maybe buy me enough time to get the fuck out of Buffalo as fast as I could.

"Thank you, thank you..."

I started on his wrists. "Don't thank me yet. You need to get to police headquarters. That's Ohio Street." I aimed my knife in the direction of the road as he rubbed his wrists and tried to pull himself out of the trunk. "Take it all the way into downtown. Flag down a cop car if you see one. Just go, now."

I helped him all the way out of the trunk. His legs were so wobbly he almost fell. I caught him under his armpits and hauled him up to size. Justin threw his arms around me and gave me a heavy hug. "Marcus, man, how did you know where I was?"

"I didn't. You got lucky." I peeled him off me. "You have to go now, Justin. Run."

I gave him a nod towards the street lights and he began to shamble towards Ohio Street. He wasn't dressed for the weather: sneakers, jeans and a ripped, bloody T-shirt. I waited until he was out of sight before I got back into the car. The temperature was dropping hard as it got closer to dusk. He would have frozen to death by nightfall.

I put the car in gear and parked it in the spot Jacki had pointed out. I left the keys in the ignition, just like I found them, and started walking toward The Bison City Club. It was a dive bar in the old first ward frequented by guys more like me than not. I thought I might find someone who could give me a ride back to McGruder's. I'd find Jacki, act like everything went as planned, and see if I could buy myself a little time. Maybe I'd have to rob a liquor store or a Quik Mart to get enough money for a bus ticket. I had seven bucks in my wallet and my pocket knife. Not much for a new life.

The snow was really coming down and there were no sidewalks in that broken down, charcoal colored part of town, so I shuffled along the side of the road, ankle deep in slush. It was hard going and my feet were wet. The bar was a lot farther from the grain elevator than I'd thought it was. The evening sky was covered over in low, thick dark clouds; no stars tonight. I bent my head into the wind and hoped oncoming cars could make out my blue jacket so I didn't end up as road pizza.

As I was mulling over the pros and cons of going back to McGruder's, the red Ford cut across the road and pulled to a stop in front of me. Karl's round face pulled back in a snarl as he blocked my path. He and Sammy Diaz were Victor's clean-up crew. I swallowed hard and tried not to shit my pants.

Sammy pulled up behind the red Ford in his SUV. He sat and watched as Karl got out and approached me. Karl had the keys with its busted shamrock key chain between his fingers. No gloves. Not worried about leaving prints.

"Tell me, Marcus." Karl waved the keys in front of my face. "Why our popsicle is sitting in front of the cops and not stuck to the bottom of this here trunk?"

"I don't know what you're talking about," I said. "I left the car right where Jacki said. No stops. All on the square."

He slapped me hard with the keys in his hand. "I knew we shoulda used someone else. But Jacki said you were a stand-up guy. And Victor wanted to give you a chance. Now the star witness in the *People versus Victor Wright* is drinking coffee with the narcotics squad, according to our snitch with the police."

"Whoever it is, they musta got out after I left. I swear. I heard the thumping around, but, hey, that's none of my business, right? I made the drop. You left some guy alive back there? Why didn't you kill him if that's what you wanted? Who leaves someone in a car to freeze?"

He caught me in the mouth again. This one dropped me to my knees. "Victor Wright does. When he's trying to send a message. When he wants you to think about what you did as you cross over into that good night." He grabbed me by my coat collar and hauled me up. "And you're so dumb you didn't even take the money in the glove box. You must really feel some loyalty to Joey. It's a good thing we had time to snag the car because Justin is such a shit for brains he couldn't remember which elevator he was at."

"I'm telling you, man. This is all wrong..."

He pulled a Glock from under his coat and tossed me the keys. "Open the trunk. Get in. We still got questions to ask you and this ain't the appropriate place."

"I'm not getting in that trunk," I said, taking a step back.

"You're going to get into that trunk or I'm going to put a bullet into your skull right here, on the side of the road."

I knew that look in his eyes, that set to his jaw. I'd seen it in dozens of guys just like him. He wasn't kidding. I turned the trunk key in the lock and popped it open. "Get in," he repeated. I knew he wasn't going to say it again.

So that's how I ended up in the trunk of this car, heading to who knows where, on the way to getting myself murdered.

I pat myself down the best I can. In my jacket pockets I got my dead cellphone, my wallet, the keys to my apartment and the pocket knife I used to cut the duct tape off the kid.

I got a pocket knife.

A really sharp pocket knife.

I feel around again. The wheel well on the left isn't smooth. In fact, it's flaky with rust. I dig around with my knife, but there's no way I'll be able to puncture a moving tire. I feel around to the back seat, stabbing at it, but I can't tear a big enough hole with my little knife to get through to the back seat. Stupid ass Ford.

I have to think, think, think, which has never been my strong point under pressure. All I got is a small, sharp pocket knife and the element of surprise. Against Karl. And Sammy, who I'm sure is following right behind us in the SUV.

I start to kick at the trunk lock as hard as I can. I brace myself against the back of the rear seat and kick straight out with both legs in my heavy work boots. Then I do it again. And again. The trunk dents outward. I kick again.

The trunk springs open, covering Karl's rear view, exposing me to the night sky and bitter wind. The car starts to skid. Sammy is going too fast and plows into the back of the Fairlane. Thankfully, I'm already pinned up against the back of the rear seat. The Ford's back end crunches and crumples. Both cars slide, colliding into the guard rail with an ear splitting, scraping shriek. Then we're sliding down, down, down. I try to hold on to the edge of the trunk, but I'm afraid the lid will come down again and cut my fingers off. The next thing I know, we're slammed again, this time from the front, and I go airborne. Then I'm out of the trunk, tumbling through the air into a snowbank.

If you think landing in the snow is a soft, cushy deal, you don't know anything about the ice and rocks underneath it. Something in my left ankle snaps. Everything goes white and it takes me a second to focus. The horn on the Fairlane is stuck and blaring. A steady wail that's going straight through my head. When I come to my senses and manage to sit up, I see that the Ford smashed grill-first into a tree at the bottom of a small ravine next to a set of abandoned railroad tracks, with the SUV pinned between two smaller trees to the right.

I start to crawl away from the wreckage.

From the SUV I hear another sound. "Marcus, you son of a bitch!"

I turn to see Sammy, bloody and covered in airbag powder, stumbling toward me.

"I'm gonna kill you with my bare hands, you piece of shit," Sammy roars, stomping through the snow to get to me.

I roll onto my back.

Sammy has an inch-wide gash across his bald scalp, blood flowing freely from beneath a flap of skin. He reaches down and grabs the front of my Carhartt jacket and hauls me up.

The pain from my ankle burns through my body like a lightning strike.

I bury my sharp little pocket knife as deep as I can in his gut.

He makes a sound like a surprised growl and drops me. Now we're both on the ground, him grabbing at the knife sticking out of his belly and me, crab crawling as fast as I can toward the screaming Ford.

Karl had managed to get the door open and now hung, half in and half out of the driver's seat of the Fairlane. He's unconscious, face in the snow, body twisted up in the car. From behind me I can hear Sammy huffing. He's still coming after me.

I reach up and pull Karl the rest of the way out of the car. The horn stops blaring. Grabbing onto the steering wheel, I pull myself up, wincing through the pain. The shamrock key chain is still in the ignition. I throw the car into reverse. I can't believe the car is still running. I guess they really don't make them like they used to.

"You little prick," Sammy spits out, grabbing at the door handle.

I hit the gas.

The car shoots back ten, fifteen feet, knocking Sammy on his ass. He scrabbles over to Karl. He must have lost his own gun somewhere in the SUV. Now he's going for Karl's.

I throw the Fairlane into drive.

Sammy's face is pinched in pain and surprise when the Ford plows into him. I knock him back a good eight feet. Then I wait a couple seconds with my foot on the brake. He doesn't get up. I don't know if either he or Karl are dead, and I don't care. They would have left me in a lot worse shape, this I do know.

I reach over to the glove box that had cracked but not come open. Sure enough, there's the envelope just like Jacki said. I was so positive it wouldn't be there that I never bothered to check for it. I stuff it into my jacket pocket and angle the car around the guys and drive forward and up, out of the ditch.

The front end is mangled, the trunk lid is sagging down so I can see out the back, but this son of a bitch of a car is still running and it's going to take me to the bus station or die trying. I don't think anything short of a rocket launcher could take this thing out.

I'm going to get on the next bus leaving for anywhere. I'll get my ankle taken care of when I get to wherever that is. I've got ten thousand dollars in my pocket, a busted-up Ford Fairlane I can't wait to abandon, and nothing to keep me in Buffalo except for the wrath of Victor Wright and a possible manslaughter charge. Or maybe two.

Will I walk the straight and narrow now? Hell, I don't even know what that is. I don't know if I could, even if I wanted to.

The cold wind feels kinda nice on my face through the busted windshield. I think about Justin and for a moment I really hope I managed to kill Karl and Sammy. I want my friend's kid to get another shot.

When I get where I'm going the first thing I'm going to do, I decide, is buy myself a new wrench. The most expensive wrench in the whole damn hardware store. The kind of wrench a man could use to restore something like an old Ford Fairlane, if he was ever lucky enough to find another one like this one.

'Cause you know, a man's gotta build his tool collection one piece at a time.

A reporter that writes books? Is that still a cliché? Perhaps there aren't enough reporters anymore to make it so... In any case Andrew Welsh-Huggins not only works for the Associated Press, he also writes about an ex-college quarterback from Ohio State named Andy Hayes in a series of private eye novels from Swallow Press. He uses his knowledge of current affairs, his home state of Ohio and writes about them in his non-fiction books about current issues and Ohio state government. One of these is about the death penalty and another about terrorism in America's heartland. In this issue of the magazine Andrew brings us a crime story with a certain international flair...

Family Business
Andrew Welsh-Huggins

Foley wrapped up that day's client meeting and left the office shortly after noon, a little later than planned. He told his secretary he was headed to lunch. She nodded and reminded him of his two-thirty. He nodded in return, stepped into the outer hall and depressed the elevator button. Waiting for its arrival, he checked his phone and saw he had a text from Alison.

Lunch?

Sorry, appointment, he replied.

Too bad. Merger or acquisition? Accompanied by a winking smiley face.

Foley hesitated and typed his response: *More a de-acquisition.*

Sounds serious. Another time then.

Another time. He added a frown-y emoticon.

He was about to put the phone away when she texted back: *Don't forget the opening tonight. Claire's insistent you be there.*

I won't forget, he replied, as the elevator doors opened and he stepped inside.

As Foley descended he swallowed his annoyance. Of course he'd be at the opening. Alison knew he didn't care for Claire, but Alison also knew he understood how crucial Claire's connections as an independent gallery owner were to the museum. Claire was not his type, to say the least—with her clogs and hand-me-down designer jeans and cotton peasant shirts, and of course her opinions on anything and everything. Alison called Claire both a friend and a colleague, though it was beyond him what he saw in her. In any case, message received, he thought. Downstairs, he joined the lunchtime crowd waiting for the revolving doors and a moment later was on the street.

He stopped at the crosswalk a block down and took his bearings. Forced himself to focus on the problem at hand. Well, problems. Foley had two tasks that required his immediate attention. First, he had to move the Lubieniecki. Move it soon and without detection. Second, he had to end things with Kelsey. End a relationship that, however fun at the time, had turned into an improvident situation, especially with his impending marriage. De-acquisition indeed. Yes, two problems to deal with. The question was could he solve both in time?

Foley liked to keep his work and personal lives separate, for obvious and not so obvious reasons, and nowhere more so than when it came to women. Far easier to carry on a relationship off the clock, he'd always found. Easier and safer. When it came to the firm, he had nothing against his female colleagues, married or not. It's just that he preferred the security of extracurricular endeavors. Take Mariana, a Brazilian professor on a one-year exchange at Otterbein he met one evening at the symphony. She professed to know nothing of the law and he struggled to understand her slice of the microbiology field. But in the ways that mattered, they were very much compatible.

That self-enforced work life divide ended abruptly with Alison. Ended to his surprise and, if he were being honest about it, to his relief as well. Though she wasn't a member of the firm or even a lawyer, they'd met because the art museum was a client—a professional connection to be sure. She a new board member, he advising the board on a series of investments. Right away, he found himself drawn to her confident face, pretty though not beautiful, and the way she carried herself with understated intelligence. Plus, her obvious knowledge of art, which in his experience was unusual in someone not directly employed in the field. The attraction didn't seem mutual, however, which puzzled him, based on his usual experience with women. She seemed to be taking his measure, in a way he wasn't accustomed to. Against his better judgment, and despite his rule against dating anyone from the art world, Foley found himself dreaming up ways to win her over.

He needn't have bothered. A month after they met, Alison invited him to a museum fundraiser in the new wing. Dressed in a simple, sleeveless gray sheath dress that set her off from every other woman in the room, she'd hooked her arm in his and that, it seemed, was that.

If Alison's looks and business-like demeanor had piqued his interest, her resume snagged him over the longer term. Art history major at Kenyon, master's from the London School of Economics, service on several arts-related boards. All of this balanced with her job as an insurance company risk adjustor, the same line of work as her father. In Chicago at first, making her own way, then recently back in Columbus as dad prepared to retire and turn over the reins to a worthy successor.

The romance that followed was not so much whirlwind as efficient, a succession of dates involving theater, the symphony and events at the university, strolls through the gardens at Inniswood on the city's northeast side, dinners in the Short North, weekend getaways to New York and then a week in Paris, at the end of which Foley presented her with the ring. A late engagement for both compared to their peers as they stared forty in the eyes. A wedding date set for a month from next week. The plan was for him to leave his small house in German Village, already up for sale and expected to go quickly and in the six figures, and move into her house in Bexley, a bit big for her but perfect for the two of them and their collections.

That left the apartment, of course. Foley puzzled what to do about it. He couldn't very well tell her of its existence, or more to the point, what it housed. He thought about reverting to the old system, the temperature controlled warehouse on the east side, but the thought depressed him. There was a special, secretive quality to the downtown address that he was reluctant to give up. The way it permitted him to hide in plain sight. The apartment came fully furnished but he had never taken anyone there, especially not the women he was with before Alison. None of them had more than a passing appreciation of art, a deliberate choice on his part. But all had cultured tastes that fit his own standards for companionship. Tastes that could have led to questions about the objects hanging in the apartment—and leaning against walls, and stacked in closets—that could become uncomfortable. Alison? The thought was absurd. The art history background that had attracted him to her in the first place made revealing the existence of the fourth-floor dwelling an impossibility. Its purpose would have been apparent to her immediately.

And then, of course, there was Kelsey. A throwback to his previous attachments. As far from Foley's day job and his, well, his other employment as possible. A final fling? That much was obvious. In any case, one that had to come to an end. Today.

The traffic light changed and he crossed the street. The temperature had fallen, still not overcoat weather but autumn was in the air. The first real Ohio State game coming this Saturday, against Penn State. He pushed both Alison and Kelsey out of his mind and forced himself to focus on the Lubieniecki. On the best way to dispose of it. Best, and fastest. It was a dilemma unparalleled in Foley's experience as a... as a what? A transitioner of misplaced art? Someone who facilitated the passage of lost paintings without too much time spent dwelling on how they'd become lost to begin with. What museums they'd been lost from. How much those museums—and sometimes the police—were offering to see them returned. He knew if he didn't do it, someone else would and with a far less delicate sensibility.

The Lubieniecki was a different story. A self-portrait by the Polish master with an ugly history that Foley had to redeem, and quickly. It meant passing up a small fortune but there were certain lines even he wouldn't cross. Normally, on the rare occasions he came across looted art, he'd take his time with the arrangements, devising an overlapping series of transactions to hide the painting's journey home, likely a trip of several months that protected all parties concerned. But he didn't have that luxury any longer. He had to move fast because someone else knew about it. Someone who cared nothing for the painting's provenance but everything about finding the best price. The person's interest telegraphed via a series of urgent texts and calls and emails through Foley's contacts that had his carefully constructed warning system flashing red. He had to launch the painting eastward, out of danger, and soon.

All of which would have been bad enough if he hadn't been such a fool and placed everything in jeopardy in the name of his ego. Old habits die hard, he told himself at the beginning, with Kelsey. Who was he kidding? There was nothing old about her. That was the whole point.

They met at the coffee shop on the ground floor of the building where she worked behind the counter. Not all that long before he proposed to Alison, if he were counting. The space had always housed a coffee shop but no one thought this latest incarnation would last. The name, for starters, Blended Beanz—simply ridiculous. And the prices—the first time he missed a Starbucks receipt. And God help us, the grumpy staff. The shop's only selling point was that its coffee was, in fact, fantastic. Rich as chocolate, smooth as butter. The rare pour of gourmet java that didn't need milk or sugar to cut its acrid bite. A vice Foley didn't make excuses for: he loved a good cup of coffee any time of day.

"I've never had anything like this," he said, taking a sip one morning after she handed him his cup. The first time he'd noticed her. Sunny and cheerful, she stood out from her co-workers like a Paul Klee in a gallery of Dutch masters. "What's your secret?"

"The usual spit and polish," she said with a laugh.

"Seriously, though. Is it the brewing? The roasting?"

"All of that," Kelsey said, smiling. Her name superimposed on what he assumed was her baby picture on an oversized Blended Beanz button pinned above her left breast. "It's the family business. It gets in your blood."

"Your family owns this place?"

"Not this store," she said, blushing. "I didn't mean that. I've just grown up doing it this way."

"It's amazing, whichever way it is," he said, and smiled and left it at that. There was no reason to pursue things, despite a shared interest in good coffee. Not that it was out of the realm of possibility, Foley told himself as he walked away. His looks—it wasn't a question of vanity, just the reality of the thing—had turned heads almost as young as hers in the past, and the consequences had not been displeasing for either party. But the skin-deep attraction of a trim twenty-something aside, he preferred adults. She was practically a kid, probably a year out of college at best. Clothes a whimsical combination of Target and upscale thrift store. Short, brown hair. No jewelry other than a single nose stud. No make-up. Most of all, no reserve. Always smiling, always friendly. A girl it would be nearly impossible to flirt with, he concluded that first day, entering the elevator with his cup of Ethiopian, because flirting required a capacity for hinting instead of broadcasting that she seemed incapable of carrying off. And where was the fun in that?

Foley walked three blocks, crossed the street and walked two more. He passed the entrance of Southpoint Luxury Apartments without a glance. A half block farther down he stopped and pulled open the door to the parking garage and stepped inside. Hugging the wall on the left, away from the lane where cars exited, he walked to the glass doors at the top of the first garage level, passed through without hesitation and turned left down the corridor toward the elevators. He paused before the final corner and opened the door to the stairs instead. He'd learned something fascinating years ago when he first rented the apartment—the building on the cutting edge of the downtown housing boom—and asked about security. The basement-level cameras captured everyone driving in and out. They also recorded images of people waiting for the elevators as well as riding inside them, a fact he wondered if the pickers and scratchers and farters among his fellow renters were aware of. What the cameras didn't take pictures of was the door to the stairwell or the stairs themselves. Though technically available to ascend and always open, they were only there for emergencies, after all. Perfect for... *transitioning* certain items in and out of the apartment.

After reaching the fourth-floor landing and pausing to catch his breath, Foley opened the door and strode down the hallway. He pulled out his key, turned the lock and let himself in. He set down his briefcase and glanced at his watch. He had cut it uncharacteristically close; only five minutes to spare. He checked his phone and saw that Alison had called twice on his walk over. Odd. But no time to return the calls now—that would have to wait until afterward. After Kelsey came and went.

* * *

At first he thought it was an accident, the day her hand brushed his as she returned his credit card, the rush of a harried retail person juggling several duties. Then Foley looked up and saw Kelsey's eyes meeting his. Smiling as always, but something different today. Suggestive seemed too pretentious, especially for her—at least what he knew of her then. But inviting in a way he wasn't accustomed to during a fleeting coffee delivery moment. Was she, even with the clear difference in their age, flirting with him after all?

He tested the theory the following morning, pretending to study his phone before making a selection so his approach to the counter was timed with her availability. Nothing in her smile betrayed a hint of the previous day. But she rested her fingers in his palm in unmistakable fashion as she handed him his change—he'd purposefully paid with cash—and let her eyes linger on his. Foley was fascinated. For the first time he acknowledged that she was attractive in her own way, despite her casual nature and dressed-down appearance: petite with a smooth neck, breasts that brought to mind peaches fitting perfectly in his hands and just-curvy-enough hips.

On the third day he used a credit card again and jotted down his cell phone on the receipt before handing it back.

There wasn't a fourth day. There was no need.

Foley reddened at the thought, of something oh-so-Pygmalion about the undertaking. But there was no disguising it. After all, it was both Kelsey's youth and seeming naiveté—yes, her blank canvas—that allowed him to risk bringing her to the apartment. But what was he supposed to do? She mentioned roommates and that ended that. His own home, firmly in the realtor's hands, was now off limits. A hotel was out of the question. Their initial encounter erased any lingering reservations that he was putting his operation in jeopardy as she undressed to reveal mismatched socks and a pair of Hello Kitty panties. A far cry from the silk teddies and expensive French lingerie he'd grown accustomed to with both Alison as well as those who'd come before her. Kelsey lacked a consciousness of intentionality which suited him just fine. Glancing at the paintings as they sipped the coffee she'd brought along—his favorite, a fair trade Guatemalan blend—she accepted his throwaway comments about "off-site storage" and "tax write-offs" without hesitation. Once in the bedroom, any other concerns vanished as after their lovemaking she stared at the Lubieniecki self-portrait, which he'd injudiciously left hanging on the far wall, and asked in all seriousness if it was a Rembrandt.

"A different artist," he said, suppressing his amusement. "Do you like it?"

"I'm not sure. He seems sad."

"But he's smiling."

"I know. I don't know why I think that."

"Art is always open to interpretation."

"I guess," she said, a look of puzzlement on her face as she reached for her coffee.

What followed was an unexpectedly sweet affair. They met once or twice a week, either late in the afternoon after her shift or in the early evening if Alison was staying late at the office or was with Claire at some event or the other. Once or twice, like real lovers, they met at the apartment early, before work. Inevitably she brought them cups of coffee which they drank beforehand as she gossiped about her co-workers and he listened, offering an occasional observation which made her laugh. If it wasn't quite a romance, it was also more than a casual hook-up—not the passion of spring but not the lassitude of summer, either.

She wasn't stupid. Foley could see that. Whether growing up in the family business of coffee shops or not, she had to have known the relationship was on the brink of ending. He'd tried to set the stage through the brevity of his text messages setting up this afternoon's rendezvous, along with the absence of his usual emoticons—heart, thumbs-up, winking smiley face. He'd also prepared an arsenal of clichés: "All things have to come to an end," "Funny things happen in life," and "I never meant to hurt you."

All true, to some degree or another. But things between them had gone too far. He had realized in recent days how much he loved Alison, how ready he was to bid adieu to a single life occasionally adorned with a companion and embrace an exclusive partnership of body and of mind.

This was the exalted argument for ending the affair. The other reason was colder and more calculated and had everything to do with the painting that Kelsey had mistaken for a Rembrandt. Foley couldn't risk her getting caught up in his plans for its impending disappearance and, with luck, reappearance a few weeks later back in Krakow where it belonged. Getting caught up in, or learning more than was good for her? Did it matter? Would she have even believed a tale of a plundered Nazi artifact and the very real and very evil people seeking to prevent its return home? Either way, enough was enough. The painting must go, as must Kelsey.

He'd been prepared for tears, anger, even shouting. What he hadn't banked on was the opposite. A soft "I understand," a few tears, a hug and a whisper of wanting just one last time with him. How could he say no? They sipped a final cup of coffee together before she led him into the bedroom. He felt wistful, but also embarrassingly righteous: by telling her upfront, he'd avoided that distasteful scenario, the paramour's post-coital break-up, delivering the bad news after a final tumble in the sack. He even congratulated himself on his rectitude, lying on his back as she rode him a few minutes later, rocking back and forth, her lips parted, her moist eyes half shut.

It took a little longer than usual for him, a fact he attributed to the melancholy he was experiencing. After she rolled off him she lay still, staring at the Lubieniecki as she had after their first time together. Foley waited another minute before preparing to turn toward her, to share a final few words. Which was when he discovered he couldn't move. A weight had settled over his limbs. Torpor gripped his muscles.

"I can't move," he said.

"Are you sure?" she said, and as she replied Foley felt something twist in his stomach. What kind of response was that?

"Yes. There's something wrong with me."

Kelsey sat up and shifted to the far side of the bed. She turned and held her hand out. "Take it," she said.

"I—I can't," Foley said with difficulty. It was like talking on a below zero day after a longer than expected walk.

"You're sure?" she said.

He nodded, now quite unable to speak.

Foley watched as she got off the bed and bent to retrieve her clothes. Studying him as she dressed.

"It's a benzodiazepine," she said after a minute, as calmly as if she were describing the day's special roast at Blended Beanz. "Some people call them roofies. It's relaxing your muscles and affecting your breathing. It was in the coffee, though I'm guessing you've figured that out by now. It won't kill you by itself. Well, not in that dose anyway."

"Um," he managed.

"It will keep this from hurting," she said. She leaned over and a moment later sat up holding a small glass vial in her left hand and a syringe in her right. She corrected herself. "I mean, hurting as much as if you'd gotten this first."

Foley shifted his head back and forth in a laughable attempt at protest. But he might as well have been a shipping trunk attempting to grow arms and legs and right itself from the bowels of steerage.

"I'm sorry," Kelsey said. "We just can't afford the risk, you knowing who I am, what I look like. It's nothing personal."

He looked at her in disbelief, the last physical act he was capable of. The smile that Foley had first dismissed as beneath him, overly chipper and girlish, and then come to appreciate, like a health nut admitting that a candy bar now and then was acceptable, was gone from her face. Nothing replaced it, neither mirth nor cruelty. A face that was all business.

She scooted toward the end of the bed, lifted Foley's left foot and spread his toes. Then she did that thing with the syringe, pushing out a couple of drops, that he'd always thought was a convention of television shows.

"It's the Lubieniecki, if you care," she said. "There's no way we could let it… go home. I just thought you should know."

She stared at him a moment, then shrugged; she would have known he couldn't reply. Foley roared inside. He thought he heard a sound but it might have been his heart crashing into his throat. Blackness took him before the needle bit.

Foley opened his eyes. His mouth was dry, as after a night of too much champagne. He was nauseous. He tried to move and found that with a great effort he could raise his head an inch or two and just wiggle his fingers.

"Thank God," a voice said.

"Alison?"

"Take some breaths, darling."

"What—what happened?" His fiancée swam in and out of focus.

"What happened is we were almost too late." She patted his left hand, her tone the patronizing one she used when he sliced himself too large a piece of cake. She was sitting beside him on the bed. Foley looked toward the far wall. The Lubieniecki stared back at him, the dark eyes reproving.

Slowly, it came back to him. The break-up. The whispered acceptance. The final time together. Then the torpor, the difficulty speaking. The glint of the syringe. *Nothing personal.* He spoke her name.

"In the next room," Alison said with a sigh.

"Why?"

"Why?" Her voice rose and lost a bit of its composure. "Because you left us very little choice in the matter." She continued more softly. "Really, dear, you've been quite sloppy. Not like yourself at all. Fortunately for us you're better at fencing art than hiding keys, or we might never have gotten to you in time. But it all worked out." She paused. "It's a good thing she's so small."

Foley was quiet for a moment. He winced at the word she'd spoken. A distasteful way of putting what he did, but technically accurate. Yet how—

"You should get dressed if you're able," Alison said. "We have a lot to do."

"I—"

"Yes?"

"How? How did you know?"

"About Kelsey?"

He shook his head. "About the, ah, work I do. The... transitioning."

"Is that what you call it? How quaint. Well, of course, I've always known. It was one of the things that attracted me to you. A master secretly at work." She patted his hand again. "A *transitioner,* if you prefer. I'd hoped we could discuss things openly before the wedding. There's still plenty of time, thank goodness."

"Discuss?"

"How to merge our operations, of course."

"Merge—"

"Don't worry about the details now. There's time for all that."

"I'm not sure—"

"Not sure what?"

"What you're proposing…"

"Darling," Alison said, an edge to her voice he hadn't heard before. "Don't for a moment think I could forgive what you carried on with her—" a dismissive nod in the direction of the outer room, "—unless there'd been other considerations at work. There's no going back now."

"Considerations?"

"We really should get moving."

"No," Foley said, something occurring to him. He tried in vain to sit up. "The Lubieniecki. That's the other thing I had to do today. I have to—"

"Don't you understand? That problem's solved. It's in the other room—what's left of her, anyway. It's okay. We found out in time."

For the first time the pronoun registered. "We?"

"Claire, of course," Alison said. "She's the one who picked up on the syndicate originally. She's out there right now… cleaning up. I gather you and she never had any business before?" She looked around at the three other portraits in the room. One had last gazed into the courtyard in the Isabella Stewart Gardner museum in Boston more than a quarter of a century earlier. Another was lost in Stockholm. A third, Oslo. He shook his head.

"I still don't understand how you knew," Foley said.

"Don't you? I thought you would have figured it out by now. My art history major? All those museum boards? In risk management at the same insurance company as my father?"

"I'm not following."

"I grew up in it," she said. "It's all in the family."

"Family?"

"It's the family business, darling," she said.

26

BLACK MASK

The Richmond City Free Press

VOL. 1   All the Stories from 1928 to 1930   NO. 1

BLACK MASK

RAW LAW: THE COMPLETE CASES OF MacBRIDE & KENNEDY

VOLUME 1

BY FREDERICK NEBEL

Crimes of Richmond City

CAPTAIN STEVE MacBRIDE was a tall square-shouldered man of forty more or less hard-bitten years. He had a long, roughly chiseled face, steady eyes, a twist of a nose, and a wide, firm mouth that years of fighting his own and others' wills had hardened. His face shone ruddily, cleanly, as if it were used to frequent and vigorous contact with soap and water. For eighteen years he had been connected, in one capacity or another, with Richmond City's police department, and Richmond City today is a somewhat hectic community of almost a hundred thousand population.

Dog Eat Dog

WHEN CAPTAIN MacBRIDE was suddenly transferred from the Second Precinct to the Fifth, an undercurrent of whispered speculation trickled through the Department, buzzed in newspaper circles, and traveled along the underworld grapevine.

It was a significant move, for MacBride. Besides being the youngest captain in the Department—he was barely forty—was known throughout Richmond City as a holy terror against the criminal element. He was a lank, rangy man, with a square jaw and windy blue eyes. He was brusque, talked straight from the shoulder, and was hard-boiled as a five-minute egg. Now the Second Precinct is in the very heart of Richmond City's night-life, hence an important and busy station. The Fifth is out on the frontier, in a suburb called Grove Manor, and carries the somewhat humorous sobriquet of the Old Man's Home. Plenty of reasons, then, why MacBride's transfer should have been made matter for conjecture.

MacBride said nothing. He merely tightened his hard jaw a little harder, packed up and moved. To his successor, Captain

INTRODUCTION BY DAVID LEWIS

Series Editor: Keith Alan Deutsch

The Law Laughs Last

TOUGH precinct was the Second of Richmond City, lying in the backyard of the theatrical district and on the frontier of the railroad yards.

A hard-boiled precinct, touching the fringe of crookdom's elite on the north—the con men, the night-club barons; and on the south, the dim-lit,

Law Without Law

KENNEDY chuckled. "So you're back in the Second, Mac."

"See me here, don't you?"

"Ay, verily."

The old station-house, blown up during the last election, had been rebuilt, and the office in which Captain Stephen MacBride sat and Kennedy, the invariable news-

New Guns For Old

*No stranger to the pages of the usual suspects of crime fiction
magazines, Nick's work has also appeared in publications like
McSweeney's, The Washington Post, North American Review, Rust
& Moth, and the Evergreen Review. Several collections of his stories
are available online and the first novella in a new series, A Brutal
Bunch of Heartbroken Saps, was recently released by Shotgun Honey,
an imprint of Down & Out Books. In the meantime, we can offer...*

Closure
Nick Kolakowski

I.

My new setup makes the work much easier. The engineering is pure
slapdash. Robby bought a second-hand vacuum robot, swapped in a
more powerful motor, reinforced its flat top with a steel plate, and
welded the VR recorder on top. But at least the machine can grind
from room to room on its own, sparing me from having to pick up
and move a thirty-pound pillar of micro-cameras every few minutes.

The one downside: a mobile recorder leaves me with nothing to
do but stand there and talk to the client.

"I can't believe he's gone," says Ellen, this morning's customer,
as she dabs her reddened eyes with a moist handkerchief. "I wasn't
there for it. That's the worst part. There's no closure."

Ellen bought the full package, terabytes of data backed up in
perpetuity, so the recorder takes its sweet time, even pausing in
front of every bookshelf to scan the spines. Its downward cameras
capture each carpet-fiber and floorboard nail and dust bunny. Twenty
minutes for the living room, ten for the small bedroom just beyond,
and another five for the bathroom, if I'm lucky. I can't explain why
I'm feeling so creeped out, but I want out of here, now.

Most sessions, I stand there checking my phone while the client ignores me. Most of them are grieving, reduced to soft lumps leaking tears, or else busy packing as soon as the recorder leaves the room. Ellen is different, decades younger than most of the clients to whom I'm randomly assigned. "What's that line from the old play?" she asks. "'I can't go on, I must go on.' Something like that. Whoever wrote that knew how grief worked. It just sucks."

I grunt agreement, anxious to avoid this conversation, but also cautious about appearing too surly. The company has fired employees who are anything less than chipper on visits. Disturbs those in a fragile emotional state, is how my boss puts it.

"You must hate your job," Ellen says, with a shaky smile.

"It's fine," I lie. "I like helping people preserve their memories. When my parents sold my childhood home, all we had left were a couple of photos. This is so much better, having a fully rendered space."

"Agreed." Ellen looks around. "I liked living here. But too many memories, now. So I'm moving out of state. Not that it'll help, probably."

I try to keep the conversation on my track. "And this job pays pretty good. I guess it beats flipping burgers or whatever."

"I used to flip burgers," she says. "In high school. Before McBell shifted totally to robots."

II.

I'm the only person on my block who takes the wheel anymore. People in other vehicles startle when they see a real, live human in the driver's seat of the car next to them, my hands at precisely ten and two, checking my mirrors before executing a lane change.

Every time I push the button to start the engine, the dashboard screen inquires politely if I'd like it to take over, just to keep things safe, and I always decline. The police told me what happened wasn't my fault, that the algorithms and the bumper sensors had everything to do with the horror. But there was still somebody else's blood on my windshield.

III.

I assume most clients treat our work as a curio, a better version of the photos my parents used to take. They slip on their headsets and step inside their old houses in order to bring back memories, or to feel a pleasant twinge of nostalgia. Sometimes they have darker reasons.

One of my clients ended up in a rest home after her children stole her house from under her. It was one of those horrible holding pens for old folks: brown stains on the walls, cockroaches building their own little civilizations in the tub drains, appliances that stopped working three Presidential administrations ago. The lady had died of dehydration with her rig on, the heavy hardware tilting her head back to face the ceiling, open-mouthed. As if conversing with angels, someone sappy might have said. The nursing home attendants, speaking to a television news crew, used a simpler term: suicide.

Afterwards I went into the archives to see her file. A big no-no, but we all do it. Slipping on my rig and activating it, I found myself in a small living room cluttered with cheap wood furniture, the shelves loaded with religious icons and small incense bowls. Nothing magical, but it had meant everything to her, at the end.

"Listen up," Robby, our tech guy, says when I return to the office from the appointment with Ellen. "We got a new software update. It's not just empty environments, now. Clients can have people in 'em, if they got the footage. You think your job is bad, I had to figure out how to render old videos in 3D."

I keep thinking about Ellen and the way she smiled when asking whether I hated my job. As my recorder beeps ready, Robby walks over to his parts-strewn workbench and picks up the jury-rigged helmet we use to check out environments before we burn them into deep storage. Before he can slip the hardware over his head, I put a hand on his shoulder and gesture for him to hand it over.

"I want to review the feed," I say. "Recorder light kept flickering."

He shrugs. "Yeah, that's a problem. You up for beers later?"

"Hells yeah. Just let me check this."

The inside of the helmet smells like greasy potato chips and cherry-flavored soda. Tapping the power button on the visor, I feel the familiar coldness like an ice cube against the base of my skull. The darkness splits apart, and I'm back in Ellen's living room, every surface rendered in atomic detail. I walk over to the mantel above the fireplace, with its large photos in silver frames. I want to look more closely at the family portrait in the middle of the lineup, because I recognize the husband.

IV.

Corporate sends us out to clients who want their old videos converted to VR. My first client, a middle-aged man with an impressive ponytail, lives in a townhouse on the West Side. He guides me into his everything-white kitchen, pointing at his phone on the counter. "It's five minutes' worth of clips," he says. "And not a whole lot of angles. I'm hoping you can work with it."

"Let's see what we can do," I say, steeling myself for the worst. Corporate has a way of sending us into the field before the software is fully baked, which just leads to tears, screaming, refunds, bad reviews on websites. I tap his phone, already queued to the first clip, and watch as another middle-aged man in a beaten-up leather jacket bends down to light a firework at what looks like a Fourth of July party in a park. I can tell it's an old clip by the models of the cars parked along the curb in the background.

The clip seems workable. Pulling out my tablet from my shoulder bag, I tap a few buttons as I ask him: "What kind of rig you got?"

"Pegasus 180," he says, pointing through the kitchen doorway to the living room, where I can see a black headset on a stand beside a plush leather chair. "Is that compatible?"

"Shouldn't be a problem," I say. "Can you open up your phone's security? It's a voice command."

"Sure," he says, before turning to speak to the phone: "Uh, device, open security."

The phone beeps, and my tablet flashes a new status bar as the software goes to work, manipulating the video like a piece of clay, bending and prodding it into new shapes. As we wait, the man pours himself a glass of water—not bothering to offer me any—and leans against the counter. "He's still alive, you know."

"Who?" I ask.

"My uncle. The guy in the video. Seventy-eight, still fit, but his mind is gone. I tried taking him to the park the other day, like he used to take me when I was a kid." The man stops, wipes his eye. "It was like taking one of my kids, when they were babies. He was babbling, not making sense the whole time. We had to go home. And he used to be so strong. I can't..."

"I understand," I say, hoping to cut the conversation short. My tablet beeps as the software finishes its task. "You want me to put him in your existing environment? We can do that."

"Please," he says, rubbing his eyes dry before walking into the living room to retrieve his Pegasus. On my tablet, I can see a flattened version of his headset's point of view, and frankly, it's amazing. The man's uncle steps into the kitchen, bends down, and lights a firework in such high-definition I can see the sparks reflect on the polished tile. Our software must have done some heavy predictive rendering to pull this off.

The pony-tailed man stands in the middle of his living room, visored head tilted towards me, tears bright on his cheeks. Hands reaching out for something that isn't there—not physically, anyway.

V.

My car is the latest model. Its dozens of sensors and cameras capture its surroundings in every possible way: infrared, visible spectrum, radar signature. You can hack into its file tree and retrieve most of that data, if you know how to remove part of the dashboard and plug in, which I do.

When I called in my favor to Robby, he agreed without hesitation. What are friends for? Besides, a lot of us at the company do weird things. It's a consequence of peeking into all these lives every week. It took me fifteen minutes to tweak her account and upload the appropriate files.

I can picture Ellen in her new house, all clean lines and brightness. One day soon, when things get lonely, she will slip on her headset and walk through her old home in its yesteryear glory, looking over the books, maybe studying the patterns of noontime light on the ceiling. And she'll walk into the bedroom and find *him* there, in his black raincoat slick with rain, a slight smile on his face: her husband, alive and breathing and whole.

He won't move much, or say anything, and that will have to do. The moments she'll never see, when my car sideswiped him, are too terrible to replay. At least this way she can say goodbye, if that's what she needs.

Actually, I have no idea if she'll get closure. But I might. That's what I hope, at least.

The man himself is back again with another installment of his column that once again brings us some of the best in contemporary fiction. The books he focuses on this time have roots in the past though, but Jeff writes with such knowledge and erudition he's got me following almost all of his recommendations. I did the same last issue. (Note to Jeff: Your column is costing me too much money.) Regardless, we are indeed lucky to have him with us each issue. J. Kingston Pierce is the editor of The Rap Sheet *(therapsheet.blogspot.com/), the senior editor of* January Magazine *(januarymagazine.com/), and the former lead crime-fiction blogger for* Kirkus Reviews.

Placed in Evidence
Non-Fiction
J. Kingston Pierce

American crime fiction claims a long and durable history, dating back to the 1840s and Edgar Allan Poe's "tales of ratiocination." But it was in the 1920s, with the founding of *Black Mask* magazine, that the domestic story of crime, corruption, and chicanery really hit its stride. Male writers such as Carroll John Daly, Dashiell Hammett, Paul Cain, Erle Stanley Gardner, and Raymond Chandler developed a notably hard-boiled style of narrative—with cynical protagonists, remorseless crooks, and conniving femmes fatales—that was distinct from the more polite, puzzle-oriented Golden Age mysteries (many of the best penned by women) then gaining popularity in Great Britain. Less confident of their security and future in the wake of World War I and the Great Depression, and unsettled by word of escalating crime (the national homicide rate jumped by forty percent during Prohibition), U.S. residents were ready for stories in which walnut-knuckled gumshoes, wily lawyers, and tenacious reporters fetched order from incipient chaos. And *Black Mask* delivered that brand of fiction in pulpy plenitude.

Although time has marched on since, American crime and detective fiction hasn't forgotten its early to mid-twentieth century heyday. Or even left it wholly behind. We're still seeing new novels churned out with settings that would have been familiar to the pennies-per-word typewriter bashers of seventy, eighty, or ninety years ago. The last four decades have delivered many such works, from Max Allan Collins' *True Detective*, Andrew Bergman's *The Big Kiss-Off of 1944*, and James Ellroy's *L.A. Confidential* to Dennis Lehane's *Live by Night*, Ace Atkins' *Devil's Garden*, Andrew Hunt's *City of Saints*, and Kelli Stanley's *City of Dragons*. There's often comfort to be found in revisiting one's roots, and the roots of America's crime-fiction genre are a-tangle with Tommy Guns and gangsters, jazz joints and GIs, starlet wannabes, gambling ships, and Park Avenue parvenus. As long as writers continue to find inspiration in the era that gave American crime fiction its first fame, don't expect them to abandon it.

Which is a lucky thing, because otherwise none of the three recent top-drawer releases examined below would have reached a publisher's desk.

Cutting a well-trimmed figure far from the cliché of low-rent

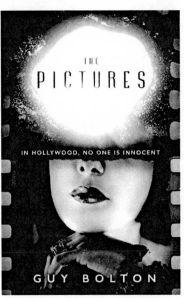

pulp heroes, Jonathan Craine—whom we meet in Guy Bolton's *The Pictures*, set in 1939—is an habitué of ostentatious Los Angeles nightclubs and wheels about California's most populous burg in a top-of-the-line V-16 Cadillac Fleetwood. What makes this remark-able is that he's also a cop. But then, *Detective* Craine used to be married to actress Celia Raymond, a curvaceous young property of Hollywood's dominant Metro-Goldwyn-Mayer (MGM) Studios, and it was through her affluence and influence that he enjoyed social advantages usually denied to brightbadged keepers of the peace. Celia is gone now, the casualty of a drug overdose five months ago; regardless, Craine's status among the chic set remains largely intact. Less sound may be his future as the Los Angeles Police Department's chief "fixer" for the billion-dollar film business—the guy who heads off trouble for dissolute actors and impetuous ingénues before the press gets wind of their peccadilloes.

Those morally dubious efforts have earned Craine approbation from the powers-that-be. In addition, however, they drove a wedge between him and his late spouse. The irony of Craine having been recruited, after Celia's passing, to help MGM disguise her suicide as an accident was not lost on the detective. It left him with a load of guilt—ponderous enough that he's more or less abandoned their eight-year-old offspring, Michael, to a boarding school where the child has lived in shell-shocked silence ever since.

Beyond that, Craine's deceptions involving Celia led him to request, as a condition of his returning to Homicide, that he be assigned *real* police work, and no longer act as "studio janitor"—a promise that's quickly broken when his division chief tasks Craine with overseeing the case of an MGM producer, fifty-two-year-old Herbert Stanley, purported to have "hanged himself in his study and left no note." Scandal-sniffing newshounds are all over this story, promulgating suspicions of a whitewash and intimating that Stanley—who'd been involved in shooting MGM's big-budget, soon-to-premiere musical fantasy, *The Wizard of Oz*—may have been driven to an early exit by rumors that his thirty-three-year-old wife, MGM star Gale Goodwin, was betraying him with other men. In this investigation, Craine will work together with Patrick O'Neill, a junior officer and the earnest son of a distinguished San Francisco police detective.

Author Bolton is a Londoner who works in the drama division of BBC Worldwide, yet he's obviously no stranger to the 1930s Southern California milieu. His L.A. claims the usual undulating palms and raised-pinky social clubs, but also slum blocks awash in tarpaper shacks and "mile after mile of billboards selling God, bank loans, and beauty creams." Joan Crawford, Clark Gable, Frank Nitti, and other period notables feature here. As far as real-life celebrities go, though, Bolton reserves most of the limelight for Louis B. Mayer, the notoriously controlling manager of MGM, who we witness at one stage sweating over whether to scrap Judy Garland's "Over the Rainbow" number from *Wizard*. While Bolton slips occasionally into discordant Britishisms, his dialogue is generally crisp. Where his film and TV background might have been most influential is in this book's twisted plotting and vigorous pacing.

From the outset it's clear that MGM, represented by its charming and manipulative head of publicity, wants to protect its investment in Gale Goodwin—even if that requires trashing producer Stanley with insinuations that he was "a depressive homosexual who'd tried to kill himself several times before." Craine is willing to repeat such hokum, at least initially. But with O'Neill pushing him to show some investigative backbone, Craine soon unearths connections he cannot ignore between Stanley's fate and the West Hollywood torture slaying, just one night before, of a fetching and suspiciously well-off thirty-year-old blonde. Then there's the mystery of the potent sedatives in Stanley's stomach, and the question of why Craine's attempt to follow up an innocent-seeming lead in the case embroiled him in an apartment house shootout. Throw in an elusive hit man, a hesitant romance, spicy photographs, and Craine's struggle to reach (and ultimately protect) his shattered boy, and *The Pictures* offers more depth and maturity than you'd expect from a debut novel. No wonder it was shortlisted for a 2017 Dagger award by the British Crime Writers' Association (CWA).

More than a century and a half after America's Civil War, the racial animus that helped spark that conflict still hasn't been purged from the nation's ethos. For proof, look only to reported police mistreatment of African-Americans over the last few years and to last August's white-nationalist rampage in Charlottesville, Virginia.

Such events give Thomas Mullen's *Lightning Men* particular currency and relevance. It's his sequel to 2016's *Darktown*, which introduced Lucius Boggs and Tommy Smith, members of a small new contingent of black policemen charged, in 1948, with maintaining peace in the crowded "colored neighborhoods" of racially divided Atlanta, Georgia. The odds of their success in that book were low, given that the police force's "real" (i.e., white) members were no more delighted with African-American cops walking beats than were average Atlantans. Nonetheless, Boggs and Smith—aided by Denny Rakestraw ("Rake"), a white officer who believes segregation should

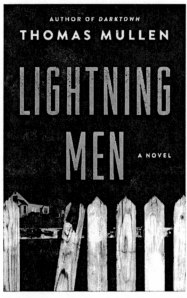

be made more fair—man-aged to solve the murder of a battered young black woman... and rid their city of a white-supremacist flatfoot in the bargain.

When we encounter this trio again, in *Lightning Men*, the year is 1950 and the Georgia capital is changing, not always for the better. Local trafficking in illegal booze has thrived since well before Prohibition in the 1920s, but now the producers of that "white lightning"—primarily pale-complexioned types from outside the city limits—are also cultivating marijuana to peddle in Darktown, the neighborhood for which Boggs, a college-educated preacher's son, and the manifestly more street-savvy Smith are primarily responsible. After a confrontation with a moonshine runner turns fatal, this pair of cops set out to identify and bring down the principal merchandisers before street fights and gunplay get out of hand. The problem is, they have no authority to question, much less arrest, white folks.

Meanwhile, Rake's Klansman brother-in-law, Dale Simpkins— convinced that his local "Klavern" has forgotten the basics of its racist mission ("Breaking bones. Cutting skin. Keeping the Negro hospital busy."), agrees to help another cadre of Kluxers demonstrate their "moral authority" by beating someone he's told is a sinful man—a sinful *white man*, it turns out. When that assignment goes horribly awry, Rake is left with the uncomfortable choice of helping his brother-in-law (a guy he thinks is "the very manifestation of lowered expectations"), or feeding him to the law and thereby hurting his sister, Simpkin's wife. It's a dexterous feat author Mullen performs, tying these disparate story lines together. He only impresses further by introducing subplots focused around Boggs's courting of a domestic whose ex-con ex-boyfriend has returned to town, hoping to pick up where they left off; and a scheme to halt the encroachment of better-off black families into whites-only sectors of town.

As excellent as *Darktown* was, *Lightning Men* is better still, a brilliant and sensitive crime yarn born convincingly from the post-World War II Atlanta black experience. Further, Mullen places his trio of cops in trying relationships that not only expand their characters, but test their loyalties to one another and their resolve to remain policemen. It's good news indeed to hear that a third book in this series is on its way.

Ray Celestin has been described as a "voracious reader of historical crime fiction," so it was not unexpected that when this British screenwriter turned author sat down to fabricate a novel, he produced a tale out of the past: 2014's *The Axeman's Jazz* (or *The Axeman*, as it later appeared in the States), based on the terrifying 1919 serial killings of at least half a dozen people in New Orleans by a never-identified nighttime perpetrator wielding—you guessed it—an axe. That novel won the CWA John Creasey New Blood Dagger for Best Debut Crime Novel of the Year, and encouraged Celestin to complete what he envisions as "a four-part series which charts the history of jazz and the Mob through the middle fifty years of the twentieth century."

Dead Man's Blues, released last year in the UK but only now reaching American bookshops, is the second installment in Celestin's sequence. It pushes clocks ahead to 1928, and shifts the action from

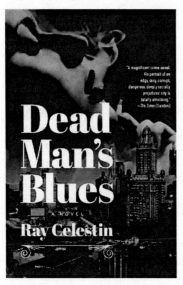

the Big Easy to Chicago. However, it employs three of the chief players from *Axeman*: Michael Talbot, a smallpox-scarred former Louisiana police lieutenant, now an operative with the Pinkerton National Detective Agency; Ida Davis, an attractive young African-American woman who's graduated from the role of clerk/receptionist for the Pinkertons in New Orleans to become Talbot's sleuthing colleague in the Windy City; and Louis Armstrong—yes, *that* Louis Armstrong—who has moved up substantially, from a boyhood playing cornet for "colored waifs" to being touted as a star trumpet musician and band leader. For Arm-strong, Ida Davis ("light-skinned enough to pass for white"), and even Talbot (married to a black woman and living in the city's once-luxurious Black Belt), Chicago provides a less-threatening home than the South. African-Americans are not altogether safe there, though. As Celestin indicates, the city in that 1920s was politically corrupt, often violent, and split along color lines, with many inhabitants convinced that the increasingly popular jazz clubs—which allowed the crossing of racial barriers—encouraged the spread of crime.

Things get underway here when Talbot and Davis are hired to find Gwendolyn Van Haren, a "strikingly beautiful" heiress who disappeared from in front of Marshall Field's on the same day her fiancé went missing from a different locale. The couple have been gone for three weeks without any word, and Gwendolyn's mother is anxious to find her—so anxious, in fact, that she's willing to pay $50,000 for her return. The private eyes are understandably skeptical of whether they've been told the whole truth about this case, but that $50,000 can't be passed up, even if it means they must leave the Pinks to collect it. While they're debating the matter, a corpse is discovered in a railroad-adjacent alleyway. The deceased is male, dressed like a gangster, and has been stabbed to death in addition to having his eyes gouged out.

There aren't many clues to what happened, but Jacob Russo, a crime-scene photographer whose hopes of joining the police force were frustrated by a leg injury, thinks this horror may relate to a previous, unsolved slaying, and initiates his own investigation. As if all those plot threads weren't sufficient, Celestin introduces us to Dante "The Gent" Sanfelippo, a New York City troubleshooter and rum runner who has returned to his hometown of Chicago at the behest of Al Capone. The mob boss wants Dante to figure out who was behind the supplying of poisoned champagne to his recent soirée for politically potent Chicagoans—and whether Capone was the primary target. Could rivals, either locally or in New York, be gunning for him?

Dead Man's Blues is a wonderfully complex, high-suspense work that explores the uneasy association between glamour, hedonism, and economic hardship. It builds on all of Celestin's principal cast, but does especially well in developing Ida Davis as a determined, daring (too daring?) investigator. Capone gets the spotlight treatment, as well, though we catch him at an inopportune turning point: just after he's been told he has syphilis, a sexually transmitted disease that will eventually result in his "mental impairment," but that for the time being—he reasons—excuses any despicable acts he might wish to commit. Buckle up!

Hardboiled, Noir and Gold Medals:

Essays on Crime Fiction Writers from the '50s through the '90s
by Rick Ollerman

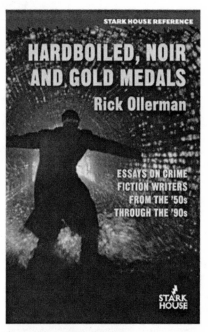

"Reading HARDBOILED, NOIR AND GOLD MEDALS is like spending a "brandy and cigars" evening with a close, trusted and knowledgeable friend as he shares the fruits of his research and the many joys of reading crime fiction. It belongs on the shelf of every crime fiction fan–as both a valuable addition to and perhaps the cornerstone of their reference books."

Alan Cranis, *Bookgasm*

"Reading one of Rick Ollerman's essays is like sitting in a master class on the writer. Having all of the essays in one collection is like getting a master's degree. This is an important book and a must-have for anybody who cares about good criticism, about the writers discussed, and about crime fiction in general."

Bill Crider, author

$17.95   296 pages
978-1-944520-32-8

STARK HOUSE PRESS
1315 H Street, Eureka, CA 95501
707-498-3135 www.StarkHousePress.com

Our featured story this issue is by one of the good ones, a man who has been writing for decades and producing numerous series across nearly half a dozen genres. Truman Smith, Professor Sally Good, Carl Burns, and Stanley Waters have all been series characters but his most enduring creation has been that of Sheriff Dan Rhodes of Blacklin County, Texas. Bill has written westerns, horror, men's adventure, young adult, all in addition to his many crime fiction novels. In science fiction writer Jack Vance's autobiography, Vance revealed something Crider himself had not known, that Vance had enjoyed reading Crider's work. His next book, That Old Scoundrel Death, *will be published next year, and he's currently collaborating on a new novel with his daughter, fellow author Angela Crider Neary, set in the California wine country called* Corkscrewed! *One last thing about Bill Crider: never get in a bar bet with him on a question of vintage paperbacks. Just... you've been warned. Instead have a warm chat about Harry Whittington, one of his favorite authors and bask in the company of one of our best.*

Tell the Bees
A Sheriff Dan Rhodes Story
Bill Crider

Sheriff Dan Rhodes was looking over some arrest reports when the call came in about the rustled bees, so he was too busy to listen in. He knew he'd find out later what it was all about, although it might take a while.

When Hack Jensen, the dispatcher, ended the call, he said, "If that don't beat everything."

Rhodes laid the reports aside, swiveled around in his desk chair, and looked at Hack. "What beats everything?"

"Bee rustling," Hack said. "You ever hear of anybody rustling bees?"

Rhodes had read about it, but before he could answer, Lawton, the jailer, came in from the cell block. He said, "Was you ever bit by a dead bee?"

Rhodes, who was a fan of old movies both bad and good, knew where that line had come from. He said to Lawton, "You're starting to look more like Walter Brennan every day."

That, of course, wasn't true. Lawton was a bit chubby, with a smiling cherub's face that was another example of why you shouldn't judge people by their appearances.

"We ain't talkin' about dead bees or gettin' bit," Hack said. "We're talking about rustled bees. You can't rustle dead bees. They gotta be alive to be rustled."

"Okay," Lawton said, "but how do you do rustle 'em? Saddle up some worker bees, round up the drones and the queen, and hit the trail?"

"You'd need you some little masks or bandanas to cover the rustler bees' faces with," Hack said.

Rhodes knew from years of experience that this kind of thing could go on for a long time if he didn't put a stop to it. He said, "Who called in the bee rustling?"

"Cisco Linares," Hack said. "He's out off the highway to Obert. Got him a lot of hives out there."

"Anybody on patrol around Obert?"

"Nope, not till later on. You might want to run out there. Cisco's mighty upset."

Rhodes stood up. "All right. I'll take a look."

"You know where his hives are?"

Rhodes had no idea. "You'd better tell me."

"He says they're on a county road just at the foot of Obert's Hill." Hack gave Rhodes the directions. "Think you can find the place?"

"I haven't been lost in this county in a long time."

"Just checking. You don't have to get snippy. Wouldn't want you to get lost."

"Don't caught in a bee stampede," Lawton said. "You got any protective gear?"

"I'm not going to be robbing any hives," Rhodes said. "Just investigating some rustling."

"Don't matter. If you're gonna mess around with bees and don't know what you're doin', you need you some protection, one of those suits and a veil, maybe a smoker, too. You got an EpiPen?"

"I'm not going to mess around with the bees," Rhodes said, "and I'm not allergic to bee stings. I just want to find out about the rustling."

"Suit yourself," Lawton said, "and don't say I didn't warn you. Did you know you were 'sposed to tell the bees when somebody dies or gets married or anything else big happens? If you don't, the bees'll die."

"So I've heard," Rhodes said.

"You remember those directions I gave you," Hack asked. "Just to be sure you get there."

"I do," Rhodes said. "My mind's not completely gone."

"Just wanted to be sure," Hack said.

As far as Rhodes knew, Blacklin County had only three commercial beekeepers, one of whom was Cisco Linares. There had been a time in Texas when a beekeeper could make some money by selling honey to the big companies, but imported honey had taken over most of that market. Now the way to make money was to ship the bees around the country to work different jobs.

Bees didn't care where they worked, and they'd become like migratory workers. In the early part of the year, beekeepers all over the country rented their bees to California almond growers to pollinate their crops. Something like a million acres of California was almond country, and every acre needed two hives of bees for pollination.

After a few weeks, the bees would be returned to their owners, who'd use them to make honey until sometime around May when the wild flowers played out. Some people still looked for Texas honey even if it cost more than the imported kind, and Blacklin County had several beekeepers who robbed their hives and bottled their own honey for sale in local markets. It was a hobby more than a moneymaker for most of them, but it brought in a few dollars.

When the wildflowers were gone, the commercial bees would get shipped off to another part of the country, maybe to Wisconsin to pollinate cranberries, and somewhere else after that, maybe West Texas for the watermelons. Cisco Linares made a decent living moving his bees around, but he couldn't make anything if he didn't have bees.

Rhodes turned the county's Tahoe to the right, onto the unpaved country road that went by Linares' property. Following Hack's directions, he drove for about a mile, turned right again onto a narrower road lined with trees on both sides, and drove for half a mile or so before coming to the entrance to Linares' land. It wasn't exactly the high-rent district, but bees didn't care about the amenities.

The Tahoe bumped over a cattle guard and into an open field. Rhodes followed the rutted dirt path that served as a road and went up over a little rise. On the other side of the rise was a small stock tank, a stand of oak trees, and what was left of Linares' bee hives. They were near the trees, and there were a lot of them, all painted bright white. Linares' red Dodge Ram pickup sat near them, and Linares sat on the open tailgate, smoking a cigarette.

Rhodes parked the Tahoe beside the pickup and got out. It was a warm day for early February, which was usually the coldest month in Blacklin County. It was in the low sixties, the bright blue sky was all sunshine, and there was no wind.

"Hey, Sheriff," Linares said when Rhodes walked up to him. He crushed the cigarette out on the tailgate and tossed the butt into the pickup bed behind him. "You gonna find my bees?"

Linares was a small man. His brown face was lined, and his black eyes had a hard shine under the brim of his hat. It was a big felt cowboy hat that had seen better days, and the brim wouldn't hold a curl. Linares's cowboy boots were in even worse shape than the hat and didn't appear to have been polished in about a decade. Or maybe two. His shirt and jeans were nearly new, though.

"Can't promise anything," Rhodes said, "but I'll try."

Linares snorted. "Won't do any good. Those bees are in California by now."

Rhodes looked out at the remaining hives. They were in groups of four, each group sitting on a wooden pallet. Two pallets were bare.

"Looks like you didn't lose many hives," Rhodes said.

"At two hundred bucks a colony for rental? That's sixteen hundred dollars." Linares reached in to his shirt pocket and brought out a package of filtered Camels. He shook out a cigarette and held the pack out to Rhodes. "Want a smoke?"

"No, thanks."

Linares turned the back to his mouth and lipped out the cigarette. He returned the pack to his pocket and got a butane lighter from his jeans. He lit up, took a drag, and blew out white smoke before putting the lighter back in his pocket. Rhodes hadn't smelled cigarette smoke in a while. Seemed that nearly everyone had quit smoking.

"Those bees are gone forever," Linares said. "Once they get to California, they'll stay there. Probably die there. Rustlers won't bother to bring 'em back, so I've lost a lot more than sixteen hundred dollars."

Rhodes thought about it. "The hives must be heavy."

"Forty, forty-five pounds, tops. A man can stack them in a van or pickup in a minute or two, easy, drive off with 'em and be gone. Man wouldn't even have to be very strong."

Rhodes looked at the remaining hives again. No bees were working, although now and then one would buzz out of a hive for some reason of his own.

"Easy pickings, then," Rhodes said.

Linares took a drag on his Camel, blew smoke. "Easy enough. You come in here without making a lot of noise and don't jolt the hives around, you'd be okay." Linares crushed out the partially smoked cigarette and tossed the butt over his shoulder. "You know what I miss, Sheriff?"

Rhodes had no idea what a beekeeper might miss, and said so.

"I miss the days when bees didn't die off like they do now. It's not like they're my pets or anything, but they need a lot more care now than they used to. When I started out, I'd lose maybe ten percent of my bees in a year. Now it's more like forty percent, maybe forty-five unless I really work at it. That's a big loss. I do what I can to keep 'em healthy, feed 'em protein in the winter, but it's a losing fight. Still lose too many. Damn pesticides." Linares slid off the tailgate and stood beside Rhodes. "My cousin Jaime and I are renting a flatbed and a fork lift tomorrow. We'll load up the rest of the hives, and Jimmy'll drive the bees to California and bring 'em back. He likes it out there."

Rhodes counted the pallets. The ground around them was undisturbed. It was too dry for any kind of tracks, and not even the feral hogs that roamed the county had come to root up the dirt. He counted twenty-three filled pallets along with the two bare ones.

Linares and his cousin would gross over eighteen thousand dollars, but there was a good bit of expense involved. Sixteen hundred dollars would have helped cover it.

"When did the bees go missing," Rhodes asked.

"Can't be sure," Linares said. "I come out here every three or four days, though, so it wasn't long ago."

"You mark the hives some way?"

"I don't brand 'em. Don't have insurance, either. Costs way more than it's worth."

Linares wasn't being much help. "You really gonna try to find my bees?" he asked. Maybe that was why he didn't sound interested. He didn't think Rhodes was going to find the bees.

"You have any ideas that might help me do that?" Rhodes asked.

"I wouldn't be wasting my time here if I did," Linares said. "My job's bees. Yours is bee rustlers."

"Anybody know where you kept your hives?"

"Lots of people, I guess."

"You ever think about getting a strong gate instead of just having a cattle guard?"

"Rustlers don't care about gates. They'd just cut the chain and come right on through."

"Good point," Rhodes said, thinking that what he needed was a clue, but although he spent another half hour looking, he didn't find a single one. And the bees weren't talking.

When Rhodes left, he had a lot to think about. It wasn't as if the theft of eight colonies of bees was a major crime, but several things nagged at him. For one, Linares' bees were well off the road, concealed by the trees that grew along the fence row and the little rise behind which they sat. Whoever had stolen the hive would have had to know where they were. For another thing, Rhodes wasn't convinced that the profit from eight colonies of bees would make hauling them to California worthwhile.

Rhodes remembered what Lawton had said back at the jail: *Seems like a bee rustler would have to know a thing or two about bees.* It was time to talk to someone who knew a thing or two about bees.

* * *

Herm Stickler lived just inside the city limits of Clearview, the county seat, and he was a backyard beekeeper. Rhodes knew him because several of Stickler's neighbors had called about the beehives. Or the bees. Just about every time someone in the vicinity was stung by a wasp or a hornet or stepped on a sticker burr or bit of glass, the Sheriff's Department got a call of complaint about bee stings. So far nobody had ever been able to prove that one of Stickler's bees had been the culprit, but it wasn't for want of trying.

Stickler's argument was that honeybees didn't sting unless somebody got in their way when they were on an assignment or when somebody disturbed them unnecessarily. After all, he'd say, Michelle Obama had a beehive in the White House garden, and her bees never stung anybody. Rhodes didn't know if that was true, but it worked for Stickler.

Rhodes parked behind a battered Ford pickup in the driveway of the old white-painted frame house, got out of the Tahoe and started for the front door. He got about halfway before someone dressed in what looked like a flimsy hazmat suit came around the corner of the house from the back. It was Stickler. He was bareheaded but carried his headpiece under one arm. He had a long-handled brush in one gloved hand.

"Don't block in my truck," Stickler said. He was a gray-haired man with a distinct Texas twang. "I just got a call about a swarm of bees that I have to go pick up."

"I need to talk to you," Rhodes said, starting for the back of the house.

"Somebody saying they got stung again?" Stickler asked, stopping to wait for Rhodes to reach him. "Wasn't my bees, I can tell you that."

It didn't take but a few steps for Rhodes to get to where Stickler stood. In the back yard under some elm trees there were four pallets of hives. The hives weren't painted white like the ones Linares had. Stickler was more creative. His were bright colors, yellow, red, green, and blue, all looking clean and fresh where the sun hit them through the elm leaves.

"Nobody got stung," Rhodes said. "This is something else, but it does involve bees."

"I can't talk now. You can follow me to the swarm, and we'll see what's what. Maybe we can talk then."

"All right," Rhodes said. "How far?"

"Not far. You know the Nelsons? Lawrence and Terrie?"

"I know where they live."

"That's the place. I'll meet you there."

It wasn't like Stickler was giving him a choice. Rhodes went back to the Tahoe, got in, and headed for the Nelson house.

The Nelsons lived in one of the older areas of Clearview, and on the way there Rhodes thought about the colorful hives in Stickler's back yard. He wondered if many people painted their hives like that. All the other hives Rhodes had seen were white, not that he'd seen that many. He wondered if the colors made any difference to the bees. Probably not.

When they reached the Nelsons' house, Stickler drove into the driveway and parked. On the side of the driveway stood an old hackberry tree that was mostly rotten. About five feet up around a big hole in the trunk a swarm of bees hung like a big gold beard. Rhodes had no idea how many bees might be there. Thousands, probably.

Stickler got out of his pickup and walked back to where Rhodes waited in the Tahoe, slipping on his headgear as he came. The headgear was mostly mesh attached to a white hat. Rhodes let the window down a couple of inches.

"You can get out and watch, and we can talk," Stickler said. "The bees won't hurt you. They're not aggressive when they're swarming. They aren't aggressive any time as long as you don't get in their way."

Rhodes looked at Stickler's outfit.

"I'm going to be up close and personal with 'em," Stickler said. "They likely won't bother me, but I do like to have my face covered. You won't have a problem. If you get stung, I'll buy your lunch."

Rhodes debated with himself for a few seconds and decided that it wouldn't be good for his image as the sheriff if he stayed in the Tahoe, and he never passed up a chance at a free lunch. So he got out.

Stickler turned and headed for the bees. "You'll have to stay fairly close so I can hear you. The bees will be buzzing when I get after them."

Tricked, Rhodes thought, but didn't say. He followed Stickler as if he'd intended to all along.

"Cisco Linares had some hives stolen last night," Rhodes said. "Eight of them. He thinks they're being hauled off to California."

Stickler had reached his pickup. He leaned over the side and brought out a wooden box and the brush that Rhodes had seen earlier.

"You think I took Cisco's bees?" Stickler asked. He waved the brush. "I'm not going to California or anywhere else. I got to catch these bees."

"What will you do with them?"

"Take them to Gary Beene. He lost a good many hives over the winter. Needs to take better care of his bees, you ask me, but bees don't care who they work for, I guess. He'd be after this swarm himself, but he's busy with another one right now."

"You and Beene sell a lot of honey?"

"Not a lot, but I sell enough to pay for my hobby. I have a few mom-and-pop stores around the county that let me put out a few bottles on a commission basis. Beene has a little fruit and vegetable stand in front of his house in the summers, and I hear he sells a good bit of honey, too."

Rhodes knew about Beene's vegetable stand. It wasn't on a paved road, but the road was graveled and easy to travel. Just about everyone in the county knew where the stand was, and a lot of people liked the idea of locally grown food and what they probably thought of as artisanal honey. Beene didn't provide everything for the stand himself. He was in business with his two sons, both of whom had property near him. One son was a farmer and provided vegetables in season, and the other had a peach orchard and grew plums, as well.

Stickler carried the box over to the swarm of bees. He took the top off the box and laid it on the ground, then held the box under the buzzing mass and started brushing the bees down into the box. A good number of them went into the box, but some of them hummed away. Rhodes stood his ground, and they didn't come near him.

"The queen's in this mass somewhere," Stickler said. "If I get her

51

in the box, all the others will follow her."

"What are the odds you'll get her?" Rhodes asked, keeping his eyes on as many of the rogue bees as he could.

"Pretty good," Stickler said. "I've never missed yet."

He worked quickly, and it took only a few seconds to get the bees in the box. Stickler set the container on the ground and put the top on it. He showed Rhodes that there was a hole in the side with something poked into it to make a kind of tunnel. Some of the bees who'd escaped the brush were already settling on the tunnel, and many were going inside.

"They follow the queen," Stickler said. "If I leave the box here a while, they'll all go in."

"How long?"

"I should leave it for a few hours. I don't have time to come back and get it, though, so I'll just have to lose some bees. Or Beene will. Some of them might find their way to his hives, but not all of them."

Rhodes thought that was a little unfair to the bees, but maybe beekeepers didn't think the way he did.

"You can follow me to Beene's place, and I'll hand off the bees," Stickler said. "Then we can see about lunch."

"I know where Beene lives," Rhodes said. "Why do you paint your hives in colors?"

"I just like 'em like that, and the bees don't mind."

"You know where Linares keeps his hives?"

"We beekeepers tend to know where the bees are. Why?"

"Just wondering," Rhodes said.

"You through wondering?"

"For now."

"Good." Stickler picked up the box and set it in his pickup bed. "I'll meet you at Beene's."

Beene's little vegetable and fruit stand was on a county road south of Clearview. It wasn't much more than a roofed counter in front, with a few tables behind it. It was shuttered for the winter.

Rhodes followed Stickler up a dirt drive to the house, which was set well back from the road, about fifty yards from the stand. The house was a relic of the 1940's that hadn't seen any updating and not much paint since then. Behind it and to the right was a detached garage that leaned to one side as if it had gotten tired of trying to stand up straight. There was no door.

Stickler drove turned off the drive and parked on the dead grass. Rhodes parked beside him and got out of the Tahoe. He looked into the garage and saw that it was a jumble of pallets and old broken hive boxes that had been tossed inside.

Next to that garage was a newer metal building, and a wide door was open on that one. Inside was a hand-cranked honey extractor and shelves lined with empty jars.

Beene's active hives were near the garage among some pecan trees. Rhodes saw eight pallets, thirty-two hives, a lot more than Stickler had. Beene must have been selling a good bit of honey at his stand. Rhodes didn't know how many of the hives were full of bees. Stickler had mentioned a big die-off.

Gary Beene was over by the hives, standing beside a box like the one Stickler was lifting from his pickup bed. Like Stickler, Beene wore his protective clothing.

"Got you another one," Stickler said, walking over to Beene with the box.

"Good," Beene said. "That'll just about put me back on track. How come you got the sheriff with you?"

In the beekeeping outfits, they looked to Rhodes like a couple of space explorers walking on another planet. He stayed where he was and looked at Beene's hives. They were white, like the ones stolen from Linares, and most other hives for that matter, but they were dirt-streaked and most of them had rotted pecans and fallen sticks lying on top of them. A mud puddle was nearby. Beene wasn't nearly as tidy as Stickler and Linares. Maybe that had something to do with his bees dying off.

Stickler set his box on the ground. "Somebody stole eight of Cisco Linares' hives. Sheriff's looking into it."

"Who'd do a thing like that?"

Stickler shrugged. "You want to transfer these bees now?"

"I'll do it later," Beene said.

The bees seemed to be behaving, so Rhodes walked over to the two men.

"I can tell who'd take those bees," he said.

Stickler looked up from the boxes. "Who?"

"I can think of two possibilities," Rhodes said. "Somebody who'd take them to California or somebody who'd keep them right here in Blacklin County."

"Kinda hard to hide a bunch of bee hives if you kept them around here," Stickler said.

Rhodes shook his head. "Not really. Somebody could hide them in plain sight."

"How's that?" Beene asked.

"Well," Rhodes said, "somebody could paint them pretty colors."

"Now just a minute," Stickler said. "Are you saying I stole those bees?"

"Not necessarily."

"Good, 'cause already told you I didn't."

"I didn't, either," Beene said. "You don't see anything hiding in plain sight around here."

"I'm not so sure about that," Rhodes told him. "Do you have a water leak?"

"What? A water leak?"

Rhodes pointed out the mud puddle. "It hasn't rained here in weeks, so you must have a leak."

"Oh," Beene said. "Yeah. I got a water leak. I been meaning to get a plumber out here."

"So you wouldn't have used any of that mud to dirty up some hives you stole from Cisco Linares."

"Nope."

"Some of that dirt looks a little shiny to me," Rhodes said. "It's on the hives with no fallen sticks on the tops. If I went over there and wiped it off, would it be damp?"

"Nope. But wouldn't you need a warrant to do something like that?"

"I don't know about him," Stickler said, "but I wouldn't."

"Wouldn't prove anything even if it was damp," Beene said. "One hive's a lot like another one. Why would I steal somebody's hives? I could just buy me some bees on the internet if I needed them."

"Yeah," Stickler said, "if you paid about a hundred and fifty bucks for less bees than we got in one of these boxes for free. You could get a lot more from Cisco for free if you stole 'em."

Rhodes indicated the garage with a thumb. "You had a big die off, and you don't take any better care of your hives than you do your bees. Get some good hives from Linares to replace the old ones, get you some bees, too, and you'd be set up for another year."

"I didn't do that," Beene said, "and I got me some free bees right here."

"Linares told me he branded his hives on the inside," Rhodes said with a straight face. "So we could check the ones you claim are yours and see if any of them are branded."

"Sounds like a plan to me," Stickler said.

Everybody wants to be a lawman, Rhodes thought, but he didn't make any move to stop Stickler when he started toward the hives.

"You better not touch my hives," Beene said.

Stickler didn't stop moving.

Beene threw the box of bees at him.

The box hit Stickler in the head, which was somewhat protected by the hat and its attached veil. The top came off the box.

Stickler didn't go down, but he stumbled into the first group of hives, sending the top two hives crashing to the ground. Stickler fell, and the tops came off the hives, too.

Stickler had told Rhodes that bees were peaceful and wouldn't hurt him, but he'd been talking about calm bees. The bees in the fallen box and hives were no longer calm. They were agitated, upset, and unhappy, and they swarmed and buzzed through the air as they looked for someone to take their unhappiness out on.

Stickler and Beene had on their beekeeping outfits, so they were probably going to be just fine, but Beene was running, anyway.

Rhodes had unprotected skin, so he ran too. He told himself that he wasn't running from the bees. He was running after Beene.

The bees were after both of them, flying, not running. Rhodes didn't know how fast bees could fly, but he thought they could fly faster than he could run. The thought gave him a little push.

Rhodes caught Beene easily, as the beekeeping outfit wasn't conducive to speed, and tackled him in front of the garage. They tumbled together into the jumble of old hives and pallets, and the bees buzzed after them.

Rhodes landed on top of Beene, which left Rhodes exposed to the bees. Beene added to Rhodes's trouble by taking hold of a piece of an old pallet board and giving Rhodes a weak smack on the side of the head with it.

The bees swarmed all around, buzzing like a table saw, or maybe

Rhodes was just hearing a buzzing in his head from the blow that Beene had given him. Rhodes grabbed the board with one hand and wrenched it away from Beene. He tossed it aside, and with his other hand he snatched off Beene's hat and veil.

Rhodes felt bees settling all over his back and head, although it might've been only his imagination. It wasn't his imagination that several of them drifted past his nose and landed on Beene's face.

Beene yelled and started to thrash like a wounded snake. Rhodes rolled off him and stood up. Beene got to his knees, rubbing his face, still yelling, and fell forward. Rhodes grabbed the back of the beekeeper's outfit and kept Beene from landing face down, although the bees that had stung Beene were already dead and wouldn't have been hurt further if Beene had landed on them.

Stickler walked into the barn as Rhodes pulled Beene to his feet.

"I see you got him," Stickler said. "Pretty slick detective work."

"That's why the county pays me the big bucks," Rhodes said. He looked around. "What happened to the bees?"

"They're out looking for new homes. Some of them might go back to their hives if anybody sets them up."

"You could do that," Rhodes said.

Stickler looked at Beene, who was slumped and looked as if he might fall. "I guess I could. I'm not sure I want to, though."

"Cisco Linares would appreciate it," Rhodes said.

"True," Stickler said.

He left the garage, and Beene said, "I was desperate, or I wouldn't've done it. Cisco has so many hives, I didn't think he'd miss any."

Rhodes thought that was one of the weakest excuses he'd ever heard, and he'd heard a lot of them.

"I need to get these stings treated," Beene said.

"I have a first aid kit in the Tahoe," Rhodes said. "I'll get the stingers out and put some hydrocortisone on the stings before we go to town."

As the left the garage, Rhodes looked over at the hives. Stickler had already set them back up, and one swarm of bees was moving in. Maybe Linares would get his bees back, after all.

Stickler glanced over at Beene while Rhodes was removing the stingers from Beene's face with the tweezers.

"So you're going to jail," Stickler said.

"Looks that way," Beene said. "Doesn't seem right to me."

"Does to me," Stickler said.

"You'd better do one thing before we leave," Rhodes said.

Beene turned his puffy face to Rhodes. "What's that?"

"Tell the bees," Rhodes said.

Uncle B. Publications & Larque Press

Pulp Modern
Vol. 2 No. 2   Winter 2018

Susan E. Abramski
Tom Andes
Marc E. Fitch
Matthew X. Gomez

J. Robert Kane
Preston Lang
Robert Petyo
Charles Roland

John Teel
Russell Thayer
Jim Thomsen

Editor: Alec Cizak
Current and back issues available on Amazon.com

Timothy J. Lockhart is a writer unafraid of the past. He's not afraid to get his hands dirty and write hardboiled stories the old-fashioned way. His first novel, Smith, *was published by Stark House Press this past June. Tim is a former Naval officer and worked in the intelligence community before leaving the service and turning to civilian law. There ain't no bunnies in the story below...*

Last Night at Skipper's Lounge
Timothy J. Lockhart

When he pushed through the wooden door, its paint more peeled than he remembered and its glass porthole more smeared, the place looked almost the same, only smaller and shabbier. The bar still ran along the left wall, tables and chairs to the right, and the tiny bandstand was still at the back too close to the restrooms.

Standing behind the bar was the man everyone called "The Skipper," only older now and more grizzled than he'd been when Mackey had come here during Aviation Officer Candidate School. The Skipper was said to be a retired chief who acquired his nickname by commanding a tugboat in Norfolk. All that was really known about him was that he'd settled here in Pensacola and opened the Lounge. Mackey had never heard the old man's real name, but both he and his bar had become legendary in the "Fly Navy" fraternity.

Although he couldn't see the Skipper's feet, Mackey knew the man was wearing mismatched socks, probably the red and green of navigation lights. The standing bet was that if anyone caught him wearing matching socks, the Skipper would buy a round for the house. In over thirty years of operating the Lounge, the Skipper had yet to pay up. After tonight—which was to be the last night, as Mackey had read in *Navy Times* two weeks ago—he never would.

Mackey stood just inside the door, looking at the array of flight suits and helmets, squadron stickers and plaques, and hundreds of framed photos of fliers. All those things and a wide variety of other items related to naval aviation—even a banged-up tail hook—covered the brick walls or hung from the ceiling. The Skipper and his patrons had obviously added to the display in the twenty-four years since Mackey had been in the bar.

Mackey surveyed the crowd, which was light at this early hour of 9:30 p.m. The place would be packed later on, both because it was a summer Saturday night at the beach and because the Skipper was finally closing the bar.

This last night at Skipper's Lounge was what had made Mackey return. He'd stayed away before to avoid running into former squadron mates who knew why he'd had to retire from the Navy after only twenty years. People who, he knew, might feel obliged to be polite to his face—or maybe not—but could be counted on to do something entirely different when his back was turned.

Mackey's flying had always been good if not spectacular, and he'd done his collateral duties efficiently enough. But he'd never managed to keep away from his brother officers' wives and girl-friends or, toward the end when more women were in the military, his sister officers—and some of those Navy women were married too.

That unfortunate trait—earning Mackey the call sign "Tomcat" even though he'd never flown F-14s—finally caught up with him when his squadron executive officer found out about Mackey's affair with the XO's wife. He made sure Mackey was transferred to a desk in a dungeon somewhere with an equally dark detaching fitness report to drag along with him. After that Mackey knew he'd never see O-5. His briefer highlighted the negative FITREP, and the promotion board shot Mackey down with a unanimous vote of "drop from further consideration."

Mackey got a beer from the assistant bartender and drifted along the walls for several minutes, looking at various display items. He knew what he was searching for but couldn't remember its exact location.

Looking at the wall, Mackey didn't see the young woman until he bumped into her, making her spill some of her drink down the front of her low-cut sundress.

"Oh, sorry. I need to look where I'm going." Mackey passed her a paper napkin. "Here, maybe this will help."

"Thanks." Her tone was cool, not rude, and she seemed, surpris-ingly, to be by herself. Mackey reflexively wondered if he might have a chance with her even though she appeared to be in her mid-twenties, two decades younger than he was.

She began dabbing at her chest, and Mackey wanted to stare at her half-exposed breasts, their tan as never-ending as the Pacific. But he forced his eyes to stay on hers as he also forced a polite smile.

When her dress was as dry as she could get it, she glanced around for a place to drop the napkin, didn't see one, and reluctantly offered it to Mackey. She saw him looking into her eyes, and, as he'd figured, decorum compelled her to smile back.

"The least I can do is buy you another drink."

"No, thanks. I haven't finished this one."

"Please—it's only fair that I replace the one I spilled. What are you drinking?"

She hesitated slightly before saying, "Gin and tonic."

"Fine. I'll be right back."

He quickly found a place at the bar and came back in just a couple of minutes. He switched drinks with her, putting the almost finished one on a nearby table, and clinked the neck of his beer bottle against her glass. "Cheers."

"Cheers," she said, looking more closely at him. "Are you a Navy pilot?"

"Was. I got out because I could make more money on the outside." He actually made less money, and unless he started doing better as a sales rep for the pharmaceutical company, he might soon be looking for yet another job.

"Oh, I see. What did you fly?"

"Hornets—F-18s." He'd really been a helicopter pilot, but he knew women were more attracted to jet jocks.

"Interesting."

She moved closer to him. She was of medium height, slim but curved with blonde hair lighter than his own medium brown. She had a pretty face set off by bright hazel eyes that were close to the same shade as his. For a moment he wondered if he'd seen her somewhere before, but he didn't think so. She was attractive enough that he didn't think he'd have forgotten.

"Were any of these things yours?" She gestured toward the wall.

"Yes, somewhere. That's what I was looking for when I should have been looking out for you." He laughed enough to keep things light.

"Let's find them. I'd like to see."

It was like spinning the dial on a safe and hearing the first tumbler click into place. That "let's" told him that he might be able to get in as long as he didn't rush things. He knew how to wait—the good hunter learns how to wait.

"Okay. I'd like to see them myself." He led the way around the room, occasionally pointing out pictures of people he knew, or some unusual artifact. He tried to sound knowledgeable without seeming cocky or even worse, boring. She said the right things and nodded at the right places, so he thought he was making some headway.

After a short while, he came to the right spot. His yellow-and-blue ball cap and his running shirt in the same colors with the class number across the front. They all had nicknames on the other side—"Mac" on his because he didn't get the other one till later.

And the photo of his Navy classmates with their Marine Corps drill instructor standing to one side. They were all in their PT gear and he and the rest of the students were smiling, but their DI looked as pissed off as ever. After they hammed it up for the camera, he made them do fifty pushups to finish that session of physical training. Seeing the photo again made him happy and sad at the same time, a strange feeling he couldn't explain.

He pointed to the picture. "Those are the guys I went through basic training with here in Pensacola."

"You all look so young."

"We were—almost all of us right out of college. I was the second-youngest guy in the class."

She looked at him, smiling again, then turned back to the photo. "And which one is you? Let's see—here?"

He looked at the face she was touching through the glass. "Yep, that's me. Aviation Officer Candidate Will Mackey. Check out that buzz cut."

She laughed. "You look better with the haircut you have now."

The second tumbler clicked. "Thanks." He knew better than to say anything more in response to the compliment. "But now you know my name and I don't know yours."

"Lisa."

"That's a nice name."

"Oh, do you think all Lisas are nice?"

"I haven't known that many."

"I'll bet. I thought fighter jocks were supposed to get around."

He chuckled for an answer and said, "Say, are you hungry? We can get something to eat. The burgers here aren't bad." They weren't good either, but he thought it was too soon to suggest they go somewhere else.

"No, I'm fine. I had something before I came."

"So did I." He'd gone back to the Oyster Reef, a seafood place he and his classmates had haunted once they were granted liberty. The dinner had been all right, but neither the décor nor the food was as good as he remembered. As he got older he noticed that nothing seemed as good as it had been years earlier, not the places, not the food, not even the women. Booze was about the same—hell, booze had always been the same—but that was it.

"In that case you probably need another beer."

He knew a hint when he heard one. "Okay, grab that table, and I'll get us another round."

She sat close to him at the table and asked him questions about his days in the Navy. She seemed to be something of a fighter-jock groupie, so he told her a couple of sea stories. Then he began asking her about herself, not pressing for anything really personal but maintaining a lot of eye contact and really listening to her answers.

She was a native of Pensacola, an only child. After high school she'd gone to Florida State for a while, but it didn't take, so she'd returned home and gone to community college for an associate's degree. She'd become a dental hygienist and liked her job well enough to keep doing it. She also liked movies, the beach, and traveling—not that she had the time or money to travel much.

"Maybe you can travel more someday. Especially if you have a friend to go with you." He hoped that remark was as subtle as he'd tried to make it but at the same time knew it couldn't be.

Had he traveled much? Yeah, sure, for the Navy. All around the world. He'd seen some of the worst places of the prettiest places on Earth. Would he tell her about some of the places? Well, okay, if she really wanted him to.

He made it good, speaking to her of taking off from an aircraft carrier and then landing on it, the enormous ship looking like a postage stamp from a few thousand feet. He told her about watching the sun rise over Guantánamo Bay, Cuba, the lush, green smell of the island coming to him on the early morning breeze. He told her about watching the sun set off Fremantle, Australia, with the unfamiliar southern stars coming into view.

She listened closely, nodding, asking an occasional question, and not looking around at the other people in the increasingly crowded bar. By the time he thought he'd said enough, the place was packed and it was getting hard to talk over the noise of the crowd. When the band cranked up conversation became almost impossible.

They'd each had about four drinks, and although the alcohol hadn't affected him much, her eyes looked a bit out of focus, and she was slurring slightly. He knew she didn't need any more to drink now, and if she wanted something later, he had a bottle at his place.

Which is where he suggested they go now. Getting too hard to talk in here. Quiet at the Navy Inn on base. He had a suite—implying they wouldn't be in his bedroom—with a balcony that faced the bay. There was a moon out, and with the night wind it would feel good to sit there and watch the moonlight over the water.

She demurred a couple of times to let him know she wasn't easy, but when he didn't push too hard, didn't try to make the decision for her, she reconsidered. Oh, all right, maybe for an hour or so. The view did sound pretty.

Despite the noise all around him, he heard the third tumbler click into place. Now all he had to do was reach down and open the door.

As they left he took one last look around. He'd never see this place again. He was leaving it behind just as he'd left AOCS behind, the Navy behind. All those days when the promise of life was still before him, when he hadn't known what he'd since learned the hard way—how the blaze of youth inevitably burns down into the embers of middle age.

Then, even though he fought against it and willed the thought not to come, he realized that he had already left the best part of his life behind and that this night would simply mark that leaving. Something made him question—and this was a first—whether he still wanted this young woman. Maybe he'd be better off if he simply said goodnight and left. Maybe she would too.

But he told himself he'd gone to too much trouble to abandon the project now. And it had been a while since he'd slept with anyone this young. Someone who, if not inexperienced, was at least not as jaded as his usual hook-up.

To avoid the hassle of getting her car on base, they went in his car. He promised to bring her back, but he didn't say when, and she didn't ask.

They didn't talk much on the way there. He tried asking her a few more questions about herself, but she gave him only short, vague answers, and he sensed she needed to be quiet for a while. Maybe she was thinking about something deep. Or maybe, after the loud noise of the bar, she was just enjoying the silence.

He showed his ID to the bored gate guard, who didn't ask to see hers, and waved them through. He drove to the Navy Inn and parked as close as he could to the entrance. He thought he might have to help her out of the car, but she managed it all right, fumbling only a little.

He gave her that Tomcat smile that had always worked so well, and after a moment she smiled back. Then he led the way to the front door and inside to the elevators. The desk clerk, an older woman, looked at them and frowned, probably because of their age difference. Whatever.

When the elevator door opened, he helped her inside and then punched the button for the third floor. Thinking of the clerk's frown, he punched it harder than he'd intended. That startled Lisa, but she didn't say anything.

When they got to his suite, he opened the door and stood aside for her to enter. She went in, looked at the small living room, and excused herself to go to the bathroom, taking her purse with her. While she was gone, he mixed two drinks, Jim Beam and water over ice, keeping both of them light.

He went to the balcony and slid the glass door open. It was almost midnight, and the air had cooled from oppressively hot to merely warm but it was still heavy with humidity and acrid with the smell of salt. He sat and admired the view, which was almost as good as he'd described.

In a few minutes she joined him. When she came out on the balcony, he stood and offered her a glass. "Sorry—no gin and tonic. I'm more a bourbon drinker myself."

She nodded and had some of her drink. She didn't seemed to care that it was different. She took a seat and he did likewise.

"Mind if I smoke?"

"No, go ahead."

She pulled cigarettes and lighter from her purse. "Want one?"

He did, but it had been hard to quit, and he didn't want to resume the habit. "No, thanks."

When she had a cigarette going, she looked out over the bay and said, "You were right—this is a pretty view."

"I'm glad you like it."

She had some more of her drink. "I'm glad you weren't kidding about it."

"Did you think I was?"

She turned to look at him. "Well, a girl never knows. Men have lied to me before."

"And one or two women have lied to me. I guess that's just how the game is played."

"It is a game, isn't it? Until things turn serious, and then it isn't." She gave him a look he couldn't interpret.

"I know what you mean." But he really didn't. Despite having been married twice—why he didn't know—he'd never been serious about a woman. Well, never serious about anything but getting one into bed.

She tapped ash on the balcony rail. "Have you ever been in love?"

Her question caught him off guard, but after a moment he realized what answer she wanted. "Uh, sure, a time or two. Unfortunately, things just didn't work out. How about you?"

She looked down at her glass, tracing its rim with a forefinger. "No, not really. Infatuated a couple of times. But I haven't met a man I could really love. I'm beginning to wonder if I'll ever meet one."

"Sure you will. You're young—you've got plenty of time."

"I guess. But my mom had me when she was younger then I am now."

"Is she still with the man?"

"Oh, no, she passed away three years ago. Cancer." She waved her cigarette. "Not from this—breast cancer."

"I'm sorry." He knew the phrase was trite, but in this case he really meant it. He had a sense that she missed her mother.

"It was bad, especially toward the end. We got close—finally— and then, just like that, she was gone."

"I'm sorry," he repeated. "And your father...?"

"I never knew him." Her flat tone cut off any further questions. She finished her drink, dropped the cigarette butt into it, and stood.

From the abrupt way she moved, he thought perhaps he'd mis-judged the signals earlier. Maybe she was going to ask him to take her back to her car. If that was it, he'd do it, he decided, instead of just calling a cab. He'd take her even though he would be disap-pointed not to spend the night with her.

But she surprised him. "It's late. Let's go to bed."

He paused so that he wouldn't seem too eager, but he was careful not to pause so long that she might reconsider. "All right."

They went into the bedroom, and he waited to see how she wanted to get undressed. Some women liked to undress in the bath-room, some liked to undress in front of him, and some liked to have him undress them.

This woman turned to face him and began removing her clothes. First her shoes, then the sundress, then the strapless, push-up bra. Finally she stepped out of her brief panties. She was tan all over, which he liked, and also shaved all over, which he always found a bit unsettling.

She gave him that uncertain smile a woman uses when she's naked in front of a man for the first time and needs reassurance. He smiled back and began getting undressed himself as she slid beneath the covers.

He'd left a light on in the living room, and that gave just enough illumination when he turned out the lights in the bedroom. He found her in the shadows and began kissing her. Her response was warm if not as eager as he'd hoped.

As a lover she was experienced enough to know what she liked and to be able to discover what he did. But she didn't make love in the absent, mechanical way he'd started noticing in women his own age.

No, this was more like when he was younger, say about this girl's age. He didn't say "girl" out loud anymore—you couldn't do that in the PC age—but he still thought of unmarried women in their twenties as "girls," and he still thought that word fit them better.

She satisfied him, and he did his best to satisfy her. Although he couldn't be sure, he didn't think she was faking when she gasped and tensed her muscles as though shot through with electricity.

Certainly she seemed content afterward. He'd cranked up the AC, and now the room seemed almost chilly, so he kept the covers over them and she snuggled into his side.

He was sleepy but forced himself to stay awake in case she wanted to talk. Some women did, afterward, and Lisa turned out to be one of them.

"That was nice." Her breath tickled the hair on his chest.

"Yes, very nice. I'm glad you wanted to stay."

"It's been a while. I hope you don't think I jump into bed with every man I meet."

"Of course not. I think we just hit it off."

"Oh, that can happen." She chuckled. "Especially after a few drinks."

She paused before saying, "It happened to my mother. She met a guy, a Navy pilot in flight training here. In fact, she met him at that same bar—that's why I went there tonight, the bar's last night. That's what she said—they 'hit it off.'"

She sounded as though she wanted to tell the story, so he prompted her. "And...?"

"Well, they were together for a while. Just a few weeks, not even months. But she loved him."

"What happened? Did they break up?"

"She said he just quit calling, stopped coming around. She got him on the phone a time or two, but he said he was busy with flight training, didn't have time to see her. You know, that sort of crap."

Yes, he knew. He'd often used work as an excuse when he'd grown tired of a woman.

"But he left her a little something to remember him by. Two things, actually."

"What?"

"One was me."

He'd seen that coming. "I understand—that's why you never knew him."

"Right. Never even saw a picture of him. She said she didn't have one, and maybe she didn't. She told me nothing else about him—I don't think she knew much, actually."

"She never tried to find him, not even to get child support?"

"I don't think so. She was a proud, independent woman. I guess she figured that if he didn't want to commit, she wouldn't try to force him to. Even if he was the only man she ever really loved."

"So what was the other thing?"

"Oh, something silly. Kind of sweet too, I guess. After they first... became intimate, he gave her a miniature set of pilot's wings."

That didn't surprise Mackey either. He'd heard of guys doing that—in fact, after he'd heard about it, he'd done it himself a few times, mostly before he finished flight training and didn't even have the right to wear wings.

But it was a hassle to keep buying the wings—especially once you'd gotten what you were after—and he didn't want to end up giving a set to some girl who'd already received one from somebody else. So he'd quit doing it.

"They were kind of like jewelry only she never wore them. She just kept them in her purse to remember him by."

She stroked his arm, her fingertips brushing across his skin. "I still have them—the only thing of his that I have."

He didn't know what to say to that, so he kissed her forehead and then lay back as though he wanted to sleep. She must have said all she wanted to say, because she soon went to sleep herself, snoring lightly. Eventually he drifted off himself.

He woke up early—all those zero-dark-thirty Navy mornings had left him unable to sleep late. Lisa was still fast asleep, maybe from all she'd had to drink, so he was able to ease out of bed without waking her. He pulled on gym shorts and a T-shirt and padded out to the bar, where he readied the coffee pot and switched it on.

He went to the balcony and quietly slid the door open. The sun felt warm even though it was still low in the east, and he knew it was going to be another sultry day in Pensacola.

Well, AOCS was a long time ago, so at least he wouldn't have to go for a two-mile run in the heat, maybe getting stuck with carrying the battalion flag the whole way. Or sweat through close-order rifle drill on the grinder, the DI yelling obscenities in his ear.

No, all that was past. Gone like many other things he'd done in his life—some of which he regretted. He'd never been one to regret much, but it seemed to him now, with two ex-wives, an only child who was practically a stranger, and his dead-end job simply a way to pay bills, that maybe a little regret was in order.

Thinking that way, and frowning despite the bay view tourists paid to see, he suddenly wanted a cigarette. For a moment he thought again about how hard it had been to quit, but the urge was strong, and he muttered, "Fuck it."

He went inside and found her purse on the coffee table. The purse was invitingly open, with the cigarettes on top of everything else, but he had to dig for the lighter. As he searched, something pricked his finger, and he snatched his hand back. Sucking the coppery pearl of blood on his finger, he opened the purse wider with his other hand and looked inside.

There was the lighter and something golden flashed next to it. He took out the lighter and then, with more care, took out the shiny thing.

It was a miniature set of pilot's wings. For a moment he was confused—if they were her mother's wings, they should have been tarnished, but these were shiny bright. The girl must polish them, he thought, probably while thinking of the father she'd never known. Resting the wings in his palm, he could feel that one of the two butterfly clasps was missing, and his finger had found the exposed pin.

The coffee wasn't quite ready, so he took the cigarettes, lighter, and miniature wings out on the balcony and closed the door behind him to keep the Florida climate out of the suite. He put the wings on a little table and lit a cigarette. The taste wasn't as good as he remembered, but after two or three drags he felt the familiar relaxation and hoped he hadn't just become a smoker again. Well, he told himself, one butt wouldn't hurt.

He took a few more puffs, savoring each, and then went inside to get a cup of the coffee. He checked on the girl, and she was still sound asleep. He went back on the balcony to enjoy his coffee and finish the cigarette.

He crushed the spent filter in the dirt of a wilting potted plant on the concrete balcony. He sipped some more coffee, picked up the wings, and cradled them in his palm.

He looked at the familiar device of a downward-pointing shield on a ship's twin-fluked anchor, thick, heavy rope looping around its top and bottom, and the strong feathered wings spreading out to either side. He remembered how proud he'd been when he'd first worn his wings, how proud his parents had been of him. Both were dead now, their best reasons for anyone's pride buried with them.

My God, he thought. This trip was supposed to be an attempt at fun, and here I am feeling lousy. I should be happy—I had a good time last night, and I proved I can still give a twenty-something girl a good time. Well, enough of being blue. We only live once, and I'm going to enjoy myself while I'm doing it.

Thinking that way lifted his spirits a little, and he toyed with the wings in his hand, watching the sun, higher now, glint off them.

Then he dropped the wings and had to scramble to stop them from bouncing on the concrete and going over the edge. He was able to cover them with his bare foot, the uncovered pin feeling sharp but not pricking the calloused skin as it had his finger.

As he carefully picked up the wings, he noticed something on the back. Tiny scratches.

The sea breeze found him, and despite the coffee and the warmth of the sun, he felt a chill. He didn't have his reading glasses—glasses he hated, having had until recently the excellent vision required in pilots—so he had to squint and hold the wings out from his face to examine the markings.

When he'd heard about giving a set of wings to a conquest, he'd also heard about marking the wings in some way. After all, some of these girls slept around, and you'd at least want her to know which set you'd given her.

Some guys scratched their initials on the backs of wings, but Mackey didn't like the idea of using something that could point so clearly back to him.

He peered at the wings, trying to read the marks that looked as though they'd been made with another pin, or maybe the tip of a sharp knife. They were tiny, but Mackey could just make them out. And that made him colder.

He tried to tell himself that the three letters could have been the initials of someone whose first name began with an M. Maybe Mike somebody. He'd known a lot of Mikes in the Navy. But he knew that the other two letters—the a and the c—were lower case. So they weren't initials.

Her hair, her eyes... Suddenly he knew why she had seemed so familiar.

Mackey stumbled to his feet, knocking over the little table and spilling his coffee. He started to go inside, then bent and heaved the coffee and everything else in his stomach onto the withered plant. When he didn't think any more would come up, he stood and leaned against the wall, the rough concrete rubbing his face like sandpaper.

He didn't move for a couple of minutes. When he thought he could walk normally, he went inside and put the cigarettes and lighter back in her purse. Then he dropped in the wings, carefully keeping their back turned away so he wouldn't have to look at those initials again.

He went into the bedroom and began picking up the clothes he'd worn the night before. Although he moved quietly, the girl stirred into wakefulness.

She opened her eyes—those bright hazel eyes—and looked at him. "Hi." She ventured a smile, which he did his best to return, but he knew it was a feeble effort. "I really slept, didn't I? I don't usually sleep this late."

"It's not too late. I mean, it's not that late. You sleep some more. I, uh, I'm going to pick up the Sunday paper."

"Okay." She yawned, stretched, and burrowed deeper under the covers. "Maybe just a few more minutes."

All he could see of her was her hair and the side of her face. He studied her profile, trying to remember.

Maybe it had been that girl who'd come to the Lounge with a couple of her friends. With the help of his buddies, Mackey had peeled her away from the others, bought her a few drinks, even danced with her some. They'd gone out a few times. Her name had been... what? He tried but couldn't remember. The names and even the faces were indistinct now, all lost to time.

All lost.

He dressed quickly in the living room. He found his wallet, phone, and car keys and eased out the door, leaving only his shaving gear and a couple of changes of clothing behind. There was nothing in the suite with his name on it, and the room was paid for through this morning.

She'd probably wait a couple of hours before deciding he wasn't coming back. She'd be angry, really pissed, maybe even mad enough to try to find him.

But she probably couldn't. Mackey was a common surname, and he'd kept a low profile on the internet, not using social media for the same reason he'd always had an unlisted landline, and, after mobiles came in, used burners to juggle his various women.

No, as far as he and the girl were concerned, this was the end of the line. Now she would have to take a cab back to her car. For a moment he wished he'd left her some money for that, but he wasn't going back. Not for that. Not for anything.

As he went down in the elevator, stomach acid burned hot in his throat, and he wondered if there really was a hell.

He pulled out of the parking lot, drove off the base, and headed west. He could be in New Orleans in less than three hours.

Back in the Navy Inn, the girl rolled over after the door shut as quietly as Mackey could manage it. She smiled as she got out of bed, still naked, went to the window, and watched a disheveled Navy pilot with a rancid soul finish pulling on his shoes as he crawled into the car that had brought them here the night before.

Then she laughed out loud. The noise sounded strange in the empty room, but she couldn't help herself. She laughed again, louder. This was for you, Barbara, she thought. All for you.

She knew she was free now, free of the promise she had made to her best friend. Her "twin," as people had referred to them since they'd been little girls.

I got him for you, Barb.

I found him. It wasn't easy, but I did it.

And I got him. Lisa only wished Barbara could know what she'd done to the son of a bitch.

Mackey had tried his old, tired routine but this time there'd been no magic to it. He'd lost his own game and damned himself forever.

She went to the bathroom and started a long, hot shower.

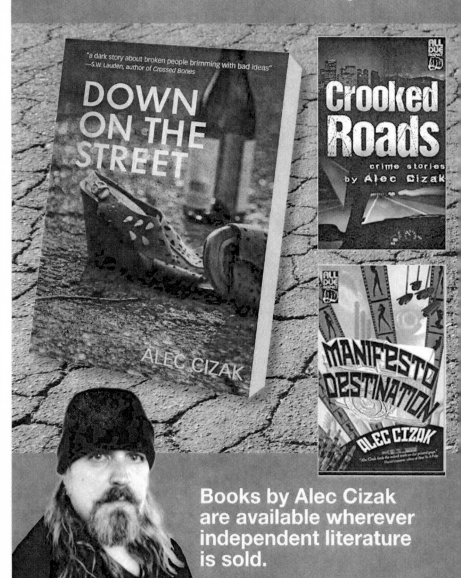

J.J. Hensley joins us as the second former police officer in this issue. He's also a former Special Agent with the U.S. Secret Service and holds a degree in the Administration of Justice from Penn State as well as a Master's in Criminal Justice Administration. Frankly, other than writing novels and short stories, I'm afraid to ask him what he's doing now. His newest book, Bolt Action Remedy, *is the first in his new Trevor Galloway series and was published by Down & Out Books. His first novel,* Resolve, *was a finalist for the International Thriller Writers' Best First Novel Award.*

A State of Decline
J.J. Hensley

Of all the ridiculous thoughts swirling through his mind, Sam was bothered most by not knowing in which state he was going to die. He allowed his eyes to shift left to the windshield and tried to catch a glimpse of the landscape through the scarce breaks in the cotton ball clouds below. They had departed a fundraiser in Harrisburg, but that had been, what? Thirty minutes ago? Forty? Sam had no idea. At this point the cities had ceased to possess their own unique script; the ink on the white page becoming smeared a little more with every new stop. For the past six months, he had spent six nights in hotels for every night he had spent in his Northern Virginia townhouse. The adjacent postage stamp yard served no purpose other than to give him a reason to break out his cheap lawnmower. Of course, mowing a lawn of any size was going to be quite a chore until this fresh bullet hole in his leg healed.

The clouds down and ahead had thinned and Sam could see the hills of central and western Pennsylvania were gone. He had grown up in the hills and always felt more comforted by the rolling topography. He knew it was illogical, but he found something horribly disconcerting about flat land. Anytime he traveled from elevated terrain to the plains, he associated the transition with that of a healthy heartbeat rising up and down on a monitor only to eventually flatten out, creating a deafening tone only he seemed to hear. What Sam saw now was one big flat line.

Ohio. He decided he was probably over Ohio. He did not want to die in fucking Ohio.

Ignoring the three dead crew members beside him, Sam brought his eyes back to the man with the gun and said, "Nobody wants to hurt you. Just put that thing away and let's work this out."

Sam immediately felt ridiculous. He was lying, of course, and the other man knew he was lying. There were *plenty* of people who wanted to hurt the lunatic—that was the nature of the business—and there was not much that could be worked out. The man had entered the cockpit, killed the pilot, killed the co-pilot, killed the navigator, and then accidentally shot Sam in the leg. It was only by sheer luck the aircraft had been on autopilot or they would already have crashed. The door to the cockpit had been locked and under normal circumstances the madman would have been stopped by the barrier, but these were not normal circumstances. When the man had approached the door, Sam instinctively had started moving in that direction. He had noticed the man's behavior becoming more erratic over the past few months and it was clear something was wrong. He had been "handled" as they say and while anyone with a rational mind could see he was slipping, few knew how far the deterioration had progressed. Sam was one of a select few who had witnessed the severity of the mood swings, the furious outbursts directed toward nobody but the surrounding air, and the debilitateing spirals into depression.

So, when the man had knocked on the door and the captain had obliged by opening it, Sam moved closer. When he then pulled a small pistol out of his suit coat pocket, Sam drew his own handgun and sprinted forward. Sam crashed into the cramped cockpit just as the third lethal head shot had been fired. Having been startled by Sam's appearance, the madman had spun and pulled the trigger of his weapon, putting a bullet through part of Sam's thigh. At least Sam thought the hot round had passed through his flesh and only taken a little muscle along the way. Being able to stand was a good sign. Regardless, he and his damaged leg were no more than four feet away from the shooter. In such close quarters, the two men dared not raise their arms to aim their weapons for fear of the other person being able to reach out and snatch the other's gun away. Rather both kept their guns trained on each other at hip level like actors in a bizarre noir detective flick set thirty thousand feet in the air.

The door had swung shut behind Sam and the man had screamed for Sam to lock it and tell the others to stay back. Sam had done so, if for no other reason than to buy time to think things through. He had been trained to expect the unexpected. But this was beyond anything he'd imagined.

"I was a pilot in the Navy, you know," said the gunman.

"I know," said Sam. "Everyone knows."

Now Sam noticed the sweat on the man's pale face. His eyes were red as if all the blood in his body had traveled there and was pooling around his irises. The man closed his eyes, making himself appear like a standing corpse, and then reopened them, switching back to a maniac on the edge of a complete psychological collapse.

"I think I could fly this thing," said the man.

Sam waited a long moment and then asked, "Where would we go?"

The man's eyes darted around the cockpit as if he was taking in some supernatural fireworks display or connecting floating dots to create a picture meaningful only to him.

Finally, he asked, "What's the next scheduled stop?"

Sam had to think about it for a moment. *Too much smeared ink*, he thought. "Waterloo. Waterloo, Iowa."

The man's disappointment was evident. "But I don't want to go to Waterloo," he whined childlike as he shifted a step left away from one of the bodies still seated behind the controls.

Sam slowly kept the pistol aimed at what he hoped was the man's chest. He had not had much practice shooting from waist level, but it would be hard to miss at this range. Of course he had two major problems confronting him. First was the fact that the man he had at the other end of the barrel might be the only other person on board who could fly the plane. And of course there was the other thing.

"So, where to?" asked Sam. "It's your plane."

The man stood, mouth agape, and Sam's heart sank as he realized there was no thought-out plan that included the survival of anyone on board. A lack of a plan meant a lack of a motive, but mass murder did not always need a logical motive. Sam knew a lack of reasoning meant there would be no bargaining, reasoning, or begging. The man raised the silver pistol and waved it around the cockpit, but kept it close to his body. Now Sam realized where the man had obtained the gun. When had it been? A month ago? How long had this so-called plan been in the works?

The silver Smith and Wesson had been gifted to the man at an NRA gathering in Arkansas, his name engraved along the slide. And now here it was, no longer in the ornate wooden box, separated from its magazine. Now it was loaded, four rounds lighter than it had been moments ago, and a few pounds of trigger pressure away from propelling another bullet into someone else's skin and bone.

The man smiled as if the greatest thought in the world had just occurred to him. "I could fly us all out of the country," he suggested. "We don't have that much fuel, but maybe we should simply head north into Canada." And he laughed wildly.

"What's so funny?" Sam asked.

The other man continued laughing and repeatedly tapped the gun on his head so hard Sam could hear the impact of metal on bone. "I didn't bring my passport. Do you think that would be a problem?"

Sam shook his head and said, "I think they would let it slide."

The lunatic pursed his lips and then said, "I should have packed my passport."

Blood trickled down the man's forehead. He touched it with the fingertips of his free hand and looked at them as if they were something foreign to his body. The broad smile he had been displaying melted away and a frown took its place.

With more concern than was warranted for a few drops of blood, he said, "I'm bleeding. Why am I bleeding?"

"You hit yourself with your gunsights," Sam told him.

"I did?"

"You did," Sam said. "Just now."

The two men stood and wordlessly watched each other for the better part of a minute. Sam listened to the normal sounds of mechanized flight.

"I don't want to do it," said the man, wiping his brow with the back of his empty hand.

"What don't you want to do?" asked Sam.

The man leaned in a few inches and whispered, "I don't really want to take us all to Canada."

"I know," said Sam.

An alert tone sounded from the console. Sam did not know anything about jets, but he assumed the tone was a prompt for the pilots to take some sort of action. Perhaps it was time to disengage the autopilot or contact whichever control tower had was in range of their communications. Whatever the desired reaction was to be, it was not going to happen.

The man was staring blankly at the horizon. He mumbled, "I'm tired of this."

"Of what?" Sam asked.

"All of it," the man replied, his eyes wide and watering. "It hasn't turned out the way I'd hoped. They were all against me from the beginning, but maybe I can start this over. I can reset all of this. When we burn, we cleanse, and the forest will regrow. It will regrow! I just have to reset the legacy. I have to reset our lives." The man's eyes drifted to the controls in front of one of the dead pilots. "All of our lives can be reset."

Sam swallowed hard, understanding the meaning behind the man's words. Over the past several years, Sam had accumulated extensive experience dealing with the mentally ill. In what seemed the blink of an eye, he had gone from a fresh-faced rookie who could not even spell the word schizophrenic to an expert at interpreting the intent attached to semi-incoherent gibberish. Irrationally, Sam wondered how he could have let it come to this. While he knew there were scores of people who could have—who should have—stepped in to stop this man, he still felt a twinge of guilt. In the beginning, the man's actions had been viewed by many as refreshing individualism. But, then the rhetoric had taken a dark turn and the rumors of drug use and abusive behavior had crept to the surface. Still, he was permitted, even encouraged, to move forward. It was all for the greater good, was the argument. Greatness could not be stopped.

"How long have you been with me, Sam?"

Sam looked at the man and noted he was standing in front of a portion of the windshield. If Sam fired, which of course was something he could not do, the .357 round would possibly travel through the man's body. Sam knew the prospect of a bullet hole causing a giant chasm to open up in the fuselage, sucking passengers out into the sky, was Hollywood bullshit. However, Sam figured punching a hole in part of the windshield could have serious consequences. *It doesn't matter*, he thought. *I can't shoot this man.*

"Since the beginning," Sam responded. "Nearly four years."

The man nodded. He raised the gun and scratched his own head with the barrel. "I wasn't wrong, you know. The media... the establishment... they screwed me over." He inhaled deeply and watched the blinking lights on the wall beside him.

Sam took the opportunity to shift a few inches to the left, closer to the nose of the plane. His leg burned with pain, but Sam did his best not to show any signs of discomfort. While he changed position, he subtly moved the gun from his right hand to his left in an effort to find an angle that would not result in the penetration of glass. Not that it would be much better if he fired into a tangle of the intricate electronics that seemed to be everywhere else in the cockpit. Not that he could imagine shooting this man anyway.

Another sound arose from the control panel and Sam could hear muffled radio traffic coming from a headset that had slipped off one of the slumping pilots. He could not make out the chatter, but he assumed some air traffic controller was attempting to make contact with the plane. The gunman refocused on Sam and noticed his sudden interest in the headset.

The man scowled and barked, "What are you doing?"

"I think they are trying to reach us," Sam said. "How about I answer them and then see if we have someone on board who can help land this thing?"

"I told you I can fly it!" the man screamed and fired a round into the floor, missing Sam's right foot by inches.

In the confined area, the noise was deafening. Sam caught himself putting pressure on the trigger of his own weapon, but managed to stop the reflex. He was starting to not trust himself. Since starting this job, his life had become one centered on reacting decisively, yet appropriately. There was no margin of error and no excuse for hesitation. But now, his countless hours of training and years of experience were creating contradictions in his mind and that mind was sending mixed signals throughout his body. There was no training for this. *The oath* had no escape clause. The responsibility was supposed to be clear.

The gunshot had caused those outside the door to start pounding on it again. It was all they could do. There was one key on board and Sam knew exactly where it was. Per protocol it was in the Detail Leader's pocket. He had been proud at the time of acceptance, but given the current circumstances, Sam was *really* wishing he would have turned down the position of Detail Leader. Sam yelled through the door for everyone to stand down.

To the madman he said, "Just calm down."

He immediately regretted having spoken the words. He was pretty sure that in the history of mankind, those words had never actually caused anyone to calm down. Sam had two ex-wives who served as proof of the uselessness of that particular statement.

"I give the orders!" the man yelled over yet another tone coming from somewhere among the myriads of buttons and switches surrounding them. "I always give the orders and they are not to be questioned. Why am I always questioned? I'm surrounded by incompetence at every turn and forces are at work—yes, Sam, there are forces working to sabotage what I am trying to create. *Forces.*"

The madman had pushed the last word through gritted teeth. His face bore the expression of a rabid dog and any hopes Sam had for convincing him to step back from the edge of the abyss were slipping away into the stratosphere.

"I'm in control!" the man said again.

Sam didn't speak. More electronic tones rang out.

"Say it!" he screamed.

Sam said, "You're in control."

The man squinted and held the gun out a few inches from his body, still out of Sam's reach. "I don't believe you mean it."

Sam stared at the man and felt an odd coolness run through his body. Even having risked his life more times than he could remember, he had never experienced what he was now feeling. For nearly twelve years, Sam had done everything possible to put himself in a position where he would be killed should his duty require him to do so. How many times had he placed his body between a threat and his protectee? How often had he pressed the gas pedal of an SUV to shield a limousine from a hostile crowd, and the passengers in the limo had been none the wiser? It was the life he had chosen and while his job was complex, there was a simplicity to the actions that he took. Protect your person at all costs. Period. If that individual is breathing at the end of the day, then you had done your job. He was certainly no stranger to dealing with crises and managing the accompanying adrenaline spikes that could send hot lava through his nerve endings. Yet here, in this cockpit, Sam was experiencing a sensation that was slowing his breathing and steeling his nerves. What he felt was a willingness to surrender to the circumstances. What he saw laid out before him was *inevitability*.

"I doubt anyone else here can fly this thing," said the man.

Sam nodded and said, "You're probably right."

Sam had serious doubts that the man, who had flown a relatively tiny F-16 during his time in the Navy would be able to fly a plane this large, but he decided to let the delusion stand for the time being.

"Did you bring your passport?" the man asked Sam.

Sam nodded.

"Why?"

Sam shrugged, not wanting to provide the answer.

"I asked you a question," the man spat as he realigned the Smith and Wesson toward Sam. "You will answer my question."

Sam took a breath and said, "Because you're unpredictable."

The man's brow furrowed into an expression of curiosity. "Why would you say that?"

Sam stared at the man in disbelief, unsure if the nutjob was trying to be funny.

Seeing the dumbfounded look on Sam's face, the gunman looked around the cockpit, at the three dead bodies, the hole he had shot in the floor, Sam's bleeding leg, and then at the gun he held in his own hand.

"I see your point," the man finally said.

More tones sounded and Sam was not sure, but he thought the plane was losing altitude. His hearing, having been somewhat impaired by the earlier gunshots, was recovering and he thought he heard more radio chatter through the blood-covered headset dangling from the pilot closest to him.

Sam asked, "What are you planning to do?"

"I told you," the man said. "I don't want to do this anymore. My legacy isn't going to be viewed as a positive one, but I'm certainly going to go down in history. Yes, I'll be remembered."

Sam watched him carefully; trying to get a read on the emotional pendulum swinging back and forth in front of him. The maniac was somber now. *My God. He's resigned to this*, Sam thought. *I really am going to die in Ohio.*

"I'll ask you the same question. What are you going to do, Sam? If you shoot me, there's nobody left to fly. But, you won't shoot me because that's against everything you're sworn to do. Yes, I know men like you. You took an oath and you won't break that oath, will you? You're like all those goddamn generals and advisors who have done everything possible to do me in. People like you... you all see things in black and white. Let me tell you what I've been telling them for years. There are no promises that can't be broken. Everything is negotiable. The world runs on deals and the ability to take advantage of those who are less savvy."

Sam watched the man who had inched closer to the controls. He looked at Sam with no small measure of disgust and Sam met his gaze with a detached and calculating stare.

"But, you don't get it," the man rambled. "People like you never get it. That's why you are who you are and I am who I am." He waved both arms as if presenting his kingdom to visiting diplomats. "People will remember me long after I'm gone. You? You're an empty suit. You're a tag-along who won't even get a mention in those newspapers you love to read so much."

The gunman turned toward the closed cockpit door and yelled, "That goes for all of you! You're sheep who stand around and wait for the slaughter. Sheep!" He then spun toward the front of the plane and lunged over the body of the dead pilot in the left seat and reached for the control stick.

The shot rang out and struck the man in the side. The silver Smith and Wesson clattered to the floor before the madman rolled off the dead pilot and joined it. He groaned and pulled back his suit jacket to expose the blood spreading on a white shirt that was more expensive than any three of Sam's suits combined. The shot had hit the man near the heart. Sam thought the man might survive, but it was doubtful.

Sam walked over and picked up the other man's gun. To his amazement, the lunatic was smiling. Sam started to turn away to open the cockpit door, but stopped. He knew it ultimately didn't matter, but Sam asked the man what he was smiling about.

"You broke your oath. I was wrong about you. You're not a sheep. You're a wolf. Good for you. A wolf in sheep's clothing is the most dangerous kind."

Sam shook his head.

"No," he said, looking out at the endless fields below. "I just don't want to die in fucking Ohio."

Sam unlocked the cockpit door and told the first person he saw to get the doctor. Sam turned to tell the madman that the doctor was on the way, but when he looked down, blank, dead eyes stared back at him.

One of his colleagues craned her head through the door and gasped. "Did you... did you just—"

"Use a secure line and make the notification," he ordered.

The doctor arrived and squeezed past Sam and the other agent.

The woman was frozen, staring at the bloody scene in the cockpit.

"Go ahead," Sam said flatly. "You better hurry."

She started to walk away, but stopped when Sam leaned out the cockpit door and said, "And ask around if anyone knows how to fly this thing."

The agent, new to the detail, ran and repeatedly shouted the question as she rushed through the passenger areas. Sam sighed, not hearing any responses to the affirmative. He retreated back into the cockpit and found the doctor facing him.

"He's... he's gone," said the man who had been attending to the madman for nearly four years and surely had expected to keep on doing so for at least a few more weeks.

Sam patted the man on the shoulder and said, "You should go back to the others and have everyone take a seat and buckle in."

Once the man left, Sam proceeded to slide the body of one of the pilots out of a seat and propped it up in a corner. He placed himself in the seat, ignoring the crimson liquid on the leather, and retrieved the headset that had fallen on the floor. He found a button he assumed would allow him to transmit, but waited to hear if the chatter he heard earlier would resume. When it did not, he pressed the button and spoke.

"Is anyone there? We are in distress."

He waited, and then heard a steady, but concerned voice.

"This is Indy Approach. State your call sign."

Sam closed his eyes. *Indy Approach. Indianapolis airport. Okay, then. Indiana.*

He could live with dying in Indiana.

"State your call sign," the voice repeated.

84

Sam leaned back in the chair and rolled his eyes at the impossibility of it all. Even if he survived this, which was doubtful, his actions would be dissected for years to come. He would be subjected to attention he certainly did not want and vilified by many. Conspiracy theorists would fire up their blogs and suggest Sam was a mole, a hired assassin. The scrutiny would be unbearable. All Sam could do was smile. *Jesus,* he thought. *Maybe I should try to steer this thing out of the country.*

"Indy Approach calling non-responsive aircraft. State your call sign," the voice on the radio demanded.

Sam pressed the button to transmit and spoke.

"Indy Approach. This is Air Force One. We are in distress."

SPINETINGLER MAGAZINE

**Edited by Sandra Ruttan
with Jack Getze**

SpinetinglerMag.com

A Few Cents A Word
Rick Ollerman

Carroll John Daly (1889-1958) was the early hardboiled superstar, the actual creator of that particular school of writing. He created it in the pages of Black Mask, *predating the better remembered (and less popular at the time) Dashiell Hammett by a number of months. Most importantly, Daly wasn't only the first, he was unique, with a loose untamed quality, the same as his character, Race Williams. While Hammett wanted to bring an almost "Pinkerton report" or procedural style to his Continental Op stories, Daly's Williams was a wild man, a holdover adventurer that charged his rates as a private investigator by the day—with a bonus per body.*

Williams had his own moral code, didn't shoot anyone who didn't shoot at him first, but was (usually) quicker and always deadlier. He wise-cracked his way into situations and while not always the brightest detective in the world, he knew how to put himself in situations that brought him the desired results. And brought him his share of those bonuses...

Daly himself was never a favorite of Black Mask *editor and WWI vet Captain Joseph Shaw. Cap Shaw much preferred the strapping characters of Erle Stanley Gardner and even Hammett's Op to the seemingly uncontrolled Race Williams. Daly had created the type of story that Shaw was looking for, but it was Hammett that gave him the style that Shaw himself could never manage in his own fiction writing career.*

But readers, though, they had their own ideas.

Fans of Black Mask *couldn't get enough of Daly's writing. Always fast-paced, always clever, Daly routinely topped readers' polls while Shaw's favorites Gardner and Hammett usually placed second and third. One of Shaw's predecessors, Harry North, said* that whenever he printed a story with Daly's name on the cover circulation went up by twenty percent. No matter the editor or whether they preferred his style or not, the fact was Daly sold magazines.

At some point, though, Daly had a dispute with Black Mask and started writing for different pulps. He created other characters, like Vee Brown and Detective Satan Hall and "Three Gun" Terry Mack. And while he was king of the pulps for years, Gardner kept churning out his many stories of Ken Corning, Lester Leith, and the likes of Speed Dash, the Human Fly, Hammett was still there with his often bloody but more sophisticated style, and then later, Raymond Chandler appeared and offered an even more sophisticated level of hard guy. Daly found himself and his creations falling behind the public's taste and he headed out west to try his hand at a new medium, comics.

There was another writer who had an arguably somewhat similar character and who took a similar path as Daly only later, in the waning days of the pulps. His showcase became the paperback original novel, even though his first book was released in hardcover although to very modest sales. This author was also a critical failure but became a tremendous success with the public. His name was Mickey Spillane.

Williams, never wealthy, was aware of Spillane's success (it was a phenomenon) and said that, "I'm broke and this guy gets rich writing my characters." But Spillane was not his own creation, Mike Hammer, any more than Daly himself was Race Williams. Spillane wrote Williams a letter letting him know that he'd grown up reading the Williams stories and that Daly had been his one and only influence on the creation of Mike Hammer. Spillane told him he wished Daly's work were still in print, that it deserved to be not only in print but in hardcover and that if there were anything he could do to help, he would.

In a later interview, Spillane says that this letter got him into trouble when Daly's agent got hold of it and initiated a plagiarism lawsuit against him. Fortunately when Daly found out about it, he fired his agent and sent Spillane an apology. Mickey's letter had been the first fan letter Williams had received in twenty-five years.

Daly's Williams and Spillane's Hammer are far from the same character: they're of the same shoot first brotherhood perhaps, the

88

action is fast and furious, but I think if the two men were ever to meet—despite Spillane's wish for the two characters to co-star in the same novel—that Williams at least couldn't help but think of Hammer as a rival with the gun. And we know what would happen then.

As far as Williams was concerned, he had no competition with a firearm and more, he had a supremely casual attitude toward testing himself. When it came to expending bullets, Williams was not shy. He was also much closer to the gentleman end of the spectrum than Mike Hammer, but Daly did come from a much earlier time. Pushing that boundary, even had Daly wanted to, would have been too much.

Creating the hardboiled school of writing was a singular achievement in itself. Often misunderstood and wrongly interchanged with noir, it is writing pared down to raw action. It is declarative, fast-moving, short on sunsets and moonbeams, long on tension and short tempers. In Daly's world his PI was a knight in second-hand clothes, a middle man of sorts, fighting according to his own set of what was right and what was wrong, not because he knew better but because the authorities were often as corrupt as the bad guys. The difference being that the bad guys usually shot quicker.

Hardboiled fiction keeps readers turning pages now as much as it ever did, which is why reading Carroll John Daly and Race Williams is still a treat today, just as it must have been all those years ago when readers saw his name on the cover of issues of Black Mask and as they were voting for him in their polls. Today, at least, a lot of Daly's is now back in print from Altus Press. As I'm sure Spillane would say amongst his own resurgence, "Thank you."

Say It With Lead!
A Race Williams Story
Carroll John Daly

Chapter 1

The man is forty-five; that's figuring low—fifty-five; that's figuring high; but he don't tell me his age. He's tall, long, and gaunt, with great sunken eyes that are steady and piercing; scrutinizing if you get what I mean. Gray or brown and then gray and brown together. The iron gray hair runs up his age, but the jet black mustache brings it down again. Thin as a rail, perhaps, but as hard as one, too. His hand is steady and grips mine tightly, which means little—great honesty, much politics, or high class confidence stuff. Sharp nose, dominant chin, hard set mouth, and you have him. Howel L. Foster is his ticket. One last bet—he has character; good or bad it doesn't matter. Here was a face you don't see every day.

"Mr. Williams," he sort of sank into a chair, "I have come from Middlend, up near the Canadian border. In a few days my life will be in real danger. I will pay you well to see that it goes no further than a danger."

As he regarded me now, his eyes seemed to drop further and further into those great sunken hollows. I nodded but said nothing. Here was a man who seemingly controlled the time of his death—or at least the threat of his death. Undoubtedly, in a few days, he would make a decision that would call for blood.

"Your integrity is beyond doubt," he went on, his voice free from flattery; just one who states a great universal truth. "I shall speak freely—hide nothing—and for once I think, put to the acid test that well known courage of yours. One lone question—" a long, bony finger came up and hovered above my chest. "After hearing what I have to say, are you in a position to act at once—within twenty-four hours?"

Fairly put—and I gave him a fair answer.

"I make no promise of taking your case," I told him. "If my job is within the law, or at least," I smiled, "within the law as I interpret it, and—" it was my turn to point a finger, "—is sufficiently honest, and has a fair figure—why—I'm your man within twenty-four minutes."

That was talking, you'll admit—besides, I hadn't exactly said anything.

His eyes never left mine.

"Good!" he snapped. "To begin with, my position up my way is one of considerable authority. We have politics there as well as in New York. Middlend and the county act when I speak. In case of trouble I can stand behind you."

Good enough—but how far behind me, he didn't say. He paused a minute—stroked his chin—then in sudden determination: "In plain words, Mr. Williams, I am a politician; also the head of a large organization of bootleggers. I have many political friends, and in a few years have rolled up a considerable fortune shipping wet goods over the Border."

I'm no nurse for a carload of gin, but I didn't tell him so yet. He had the cards; let him play them. If he read anything in my face, he was welcome to it. He waited for my question that didn't come—then he spilled the works.

"As I said—the law is my friend, but a new factor has stepped in. Hijackers."

"And you want me to protect you from them," I cut in.

What was the use of his wasting my time? That wasn't my line. What he needed was a cheap gunman.

"No!" He went on hurriedly, reading the decision in my words. "Listen—I have defied these crooks—refused to be blackmailed— hired strong, quick men, one in particular—" he leaned forward now, tapping me on the knee, "—a man to be feared—one to test the courage of even Race Williams—Sticker Haddock."

Soft and low he let the name out.

If he expected me to roll over and play dead, he was disappointed. Oh, I had heard of Haddock. "The Shooting Fool" they called him on the Avenue. He lived up to his name—went West and shot himself into stir for the whole works. The last I heard of him, he was doing life for a playful bit of murder. I told Foster so.

"Just so." He nodded. "I had him pardoned—the judge who convicted him made the appeal. I wanted Haddock with me. I got him." Those long, bony fingers clasped together. "He's my chauffeur, my confidential man. I've paid him big—trusted him—and now he has betrayed me. Within the last few days I have discovered beyond a doubt that he is working with a band of hijackers, if he is not the actual leader. He gives them information as to the time and routes of my trucks. I have been losing a fortune and dare not act. Now—"

I thought I saw the whole game as I butted in.

"Why don't you give him the gate? Blackmail?"

"Fear." He raised his head as he uttered the word. "The day I fire him, I can no longer call my life my own. This is the first man that I have ever feared. Haddock is a killer."

"Frame him—ship him back to jail."

Again came the shake of his head.

"He knows too much for that. Free, he don't dare talk, and—"

"And dead, he can't." I came to my feet. "I do a bit of shooting, all right, Mr. Foster—but I'm no hired murderer. Besides, you can get a dozen lads to plug this Haddock in the back for half my figure."

"That is not the question." He too came to his feet and deep in those sockets his eyes blazed. "I have defied the law—yes. But I play a safe game. Howel L. Foster does not have men shot in the back. I know little of a gun. To have you with me—to let him see you—to guess your purpose in being in town might be enough. But I would expect you to shoot to protect me—and later, perhaps, to avenge me."

I whistled softly. This man felt the approach of death. And he was right—Haddock was a bad actor—none worse. But it was not my game. It was an old story to me. Many an easy-going bootlegger had hired gunmen to protect him—gunmen who sold out to the hijackers. No law there—just the law of the gun. Not in my line. I started to open up when he broke in again.

"You too fear Haddock—and I don't blame you."

Though his voice was soft, his lips curled into a sneer. But I'm too old for that stuff—"Sticks and stones will break my bones" was written for children; but, it still goes for me. However, I half turned and ripped his arguing up the back.

"Your game's a dead one." I give him the glassy eye. "If you get bumped off, where do I fit? Oh, I might take it out on Haddock for punching holes in my meal ticket—but that comes under the head of pleasure, not business. I'm all business."

His eyes were narrow and shrewd now—two distant slits. You had to admire the man. Haddock was a killer. This Foster was marked for death, yet he was cold enough to lean up against a gas heater and freeze the boiler.

"Race Williams," he was playing his last card and I knew it, "come what may, I'll fire Haddock. But—by God—Haddock won't dare kill me. Death—or justice—or just fear, horror of the price of his crime will be over his head. He won't *dare* to kill me."

Pretty and dramatic; yes, but it didn't give me the expected thrill. I almost looked up at Foster and winked, but I didn't; there was something in his face that held me—something behind those crafty eyes. And this time when he spoke he said something—a real mouthful of wisdom.

"If I die." His finger came slowly out and sought the third button of my vest. "If I am murdered, I leave a will." He paused and smacked his lips. "The man who captures my slayer—dead or alive—will receive two hundred thousand dollars."

His hand just circled through the air and came down on the desk before me.

Oh, I was on my feet looking at him now. The thing was new, the thing was clever; but most of all it was reasonable. It was my turn to smack my lips. And Foster saw the change come over me. I didn't try to hide my expression. It's always better to be dragged in than to jump in. More money, if you get what I mean.

"See the point?" His hand was on my shoulder now and he was talking rapidly. "You will come with me. Haddock will see you—understand your purpose there as soon as I fire him—and let him know just what's in my will. He wouldn't *dare* kill me, knowing there would be two hundred thousand dollars waiting for the man who got him—and that Race Williams was interested in the case."

I've got to admit that here was a new interest—a most compelling interest. Still it might be better policy to wait around till

Foster got himself bumped off, then step in—croak the murderer—men like Haddock aren't captured alive—and collect. Yet—it wouldn't advertise my business—people would know I had refused the case.

"How many know about this will?" I was thinking hard.

"Just my lawyer, myself—and now you." Another long searching gaze, then, "And Haddock when I fire him."

"If you live, what?"

Man! I'll admit I was toppling—two hundred thousand dollars is real money—and Haddock was a real gunman.

"I'll tell you," he said suddenly. "I'll give you a thousand dollars now—just to come up and hang around Middlend for a few days. What say? Your fear of Haddock isn't that bad?"

What do you think? Oh, I took it—grabbed the bills and reached for my hat. This fear of Haddock talk was—well, it didn't give me an appetite.

One hour later, we had grabbed off two lowers and were making the trip to Middlend like a couple of brothers.

Dead or alive, Howel L. Foster was money in the bank.

Chapter 2

That ride produced some talk on bootleggers and a letter to Max Stern—Foster's most trusted driver of his precious trucks, in case I wanted to check up on the activities of Sticker Haddock.

Queer duck was Howel L. It couldn't be possible that he didn't trust me—yet he trusted no one. My job was simply to hang around the town—lay close when he gave Sticker Haddock the gate, and let it become generally known that in case of Foster's murder, I would work on the case. I was to park myself at the hotel. Foster slept alone in his big house—just one servant, who went home every night. He even ate his breakfast out. For my part, I had the run of the town—just bum around and get a line on who Haddock's little playmates were.

Besides, I had work of my own. Foster was a big man in his own estimation. How big he really was, I wanted to find out. So that night when I left him, I slipped around to the Police Station. Foster had wised them up that I was a friend of his, and Chief Lahley received me with open arms. And open arms with Lahley was some reception. He was big enough to embrace the Leaning Tower of Pisa and straighten it out. He had an honest face and a shock of white hair that slipped all over his roof like a mop. A Chief of Police! Why, in civilian clothes, anyone might have mistaken him for an honest man, and I dare say he was in everything but what his job depended on.

And Foster hadn't over-rated his importance so far as these birds were concerned. Every time you mentioned the big boss's name, they did everything but get up and bow. The Chief would frown when I jokingly spoke of bootleggers and hijackers. He didn't like being considered crooked, but I guess his wife and family, to say nothing of a couple of apartment houses, came first.

He'd just sit there and beam on me, and wonder where I fitted into the picture, but didn't dare ask. His hands would come together, the fingers touching one another slowly, and then he'd start his fingers working all over again. A big, good natured Saint Bernard was what—

"Cling!" Like that the telephone rang. Lahley placed his cigar carefully in the corner of his mouth, tucked in his cuffs and picked up the receiver.

"Well, what do you want?"

His voice shot out like the roar of a bull. So many complaints lately that he didn't encourage the calling of the police, I guess. But his attitude didn't last long—the red sunk from his cheeks—went from white to pasty yellow—and the cigar slipped from his fallen jaw and rolled to the floor. Then—

"What—Mr. Foster—I say—" Dropping the receiver and turning to me, "He's cut off—"

"Who? Foster? What did he say?"

I grabbed him by the shoulder. He had brains all right but they were like cough medicine—shake well before using.

"It's Foster," he finally gasped. "Someone trying to kill him, I guess. 'Help! Come quick! Help!' he kept muttering."

I got the Chief into action all right, but I couldn't get any sense out of him. Just that Foster had called for help was all he would say.

It was eleven o'clock when we slipped from the Police Station into the Ford. Lahley thought that Foster was dead—and me—well, I agreed with him inside, though I made no chirp. He sure was rattled and bent on doing the thing right. He figured it was hijackers.

Three cops already in the car, and this lumbering giant stopped to pick up two more off their beats. Another joined on the run as we turned into the grounds of Foster's house.

The house was set far back—no trees just around it. A huge stone affair—great ledges—thick vines and overhanging eaves that threw the whole dismal structure into darker shadows. But below the front windows the moon shed a dull brilliancy upon the flower-bed.

I knew the grounds and the house—been well over them that afternoon with Foster. Now, as we stopped by the door, I glanced up at the Big Boss's window, looking for a light.

The Chief had the same idea, for we both spoke together as we plainly saw the white chest and arms of the night-shirted figure at the window.

"Foster!"

"And safe," the Chief added.

I guess he was more relieved than I was.

The figure above was reassuring. This cool, unemotional man had had a real fright, and no mistake. Dimly he seemed to sway in the window as he tossed something down to us. I spotted it at once as it hurtled from the shadows into the moonlight—a key. The key to the front door.

Lahley wanted to play Romeo and Juliet for a while, but I shoved him up the steps. It was plain that Foster didn't want to talk, for fear of someone overhearing—or was he too frightened to talk? Either way, our place was in the house—up in that room beside him.

It was tough work getting that key in the lock with so many harnessed bulls crowding behind me. You couldn't tell if they wanted to help, or wanted to get in out of the dark. They had been bad enough in the Ford, but in that stuffy vestibule it was worse. Then Lahley got his bearings and chased four of them outside to surround the house.

I tell you, we made tracks to Foster's room, up the stairs—right through the little study, and bang up against his bed-room door. Lahley and I brought up sharp. The door's locked. The two cops stand behind us, switching from one leg to the other and slipping their guns nervously from left to right hand. Nice babies to have behind. Any minute I expect one of them to put a bullet in my back. But the Chief's larger, and that's some satisfaction.

Lahley pounds on the door, guesses that Foster is dead and then knows—different. The door suddenly swings open. White nightie, bleary eyes, bare feet—and Foster speaks.

"What the hell do you want?"

And Lahley does a seventeenth-century bow. He opens his mouth—gasps—rubs at his great stomach, and finally blurts out weakly, "You telephoned—for help."

"Telephoned—you fool—I—"

Then, his eyes rising and taking in the uniformed men behind, he paused; his head kind of straightened as he fought down his temper. When he spoke again his voice was as cold as a grave digger's shovel.

"I never telephoned you for help. And if I needed help, you'd be the last one I'd call on." And his eyes suddenly switching to me. "Hello, Williams—what's all the row about?"

He can't glare me down, and I don't know any curtsies. So I give him the dope.

"Telephone to the Police Station—man asks for help—says he is you—and—"

But it's a cinch he didn't telephone. One look at his map tells me that. It's as blank as an English joke. Still, the thing was rather stunning—kind of knocked me over.

"But the key—you slipped it out the window—you know."

I half gasped, for the look on his face was far from home.

"What key—I threw no key." Then catching the blank looks on our faces. "I've been asleep since ten o'clock—I don't quite understand. I never telephoned, and I never threw a key down—out a window."

Was he lying? But what else could I think—still his face—but Lahley was talking—slinging question after question at him. When things got too hot for Lahley, I horned in. Foster couldn't brow-beat me. After a bit, things cleared up and we got a pretty story. It rang with truth, too. Why? Mostly because Foster had nothing to gain by lying—and besides he had paid me one grand to protect him, not listen to fairy stories.

Listen—get this; Foster never telephoned; Foster never threw the key down; Foster had never even been at the window, and he had never even suspected that we were at the house until we pounded on the door. He'd been fast asleep since ten o'clock.

"Someone was in your room then—"

I stepped by him, gun drawn, and searched the bed-room. A bed and a closet—no other place to hide a cat in. One window—that took a rise out of me—heavy bars ran from base to top. And the door—there was a bolt there, as long as your forearm and as thick as Lahley's head. No keyhole on the outside either. I ain't a story book detective, so I'm willing to listen to the others. And their ideas of how it all happened are as interesting and as intelligent as a two-year-old at a crossword puzzle.

As for me, I'm looking over every inch of that room. Someone had thrown a key from in there. Trap doors went out when prohibition came in, and ancient passages from the time of William the Conqueror ain't found in a house built during the last twenty or thirty years. Besides, trap doors don't suddenly appear in your own bed-room.

I looked up with a start. There's an addition to our little party. I've never seen him before but I've lamped his picture hanging on a wall back in the city. He's changed some but not for the better—a horse must have kicked him in the face since I last saw his map in the Rogues' Gallery—leastwise his nose had gone and flattened up and got itself spread about his face.

It's Sticker Haddock, but he ain't a fish. A cruel, cold, calculate-ing gunman, this. He does his shooting first and his arguing after-ward. Our eyes meet as I crawl from under the bed.

"Could this be the party you're suspecting?"

He jerked a thumb contemptuously at me. I see he hasn't alto-gether broken himself of the habit of shooting his words through the side of his mouth—and he's got a big enough mouth to shoot them out any place.

He knows me all right. There aren't many crooks living who don't, I guess. Haddock's too clever to let me blow into town with-out his being wised to it. So we face each other—this sure-fire gun-man and me. He's the man I'm supposed to fear. Get that laugh? Not that I don't respect him. He's put out some pretty fast men in his day, but then—so have I.

Foster takes in the picture and does the honors; Haddock's hand comes out, and after spitting on mine for luck, I mitt him.

"I'm glad to shake hands with you—always glad to meet—" Haddock hesitates—curls up his lip; then very low, "—certain people."

And that was all of that. A threat certainly—just for the moment—the next he was a good fellow, patting Lahley on the back and telling him he was always a stickler for duty, cheering up Foster and getting over the impression to Lahley anyway, that he and Foster were the best of pals. As for me—well—Haddock smiled at me, a superior sort of smile. It was funny in a way. I could only think—what's the difference how cock-sure a lad acts? A gunman or a preacher; a killer or a professor—when a lad gets a bit of lead in him, he turns up his toes and does his stuff no matter what his training has been.

Chapter 3

There's all kinds of guesses as to just what happened. Lahley rings up the central office and soon gets the information that the call came from Foster's house. Laugh that one off. Now, if someone was bent on putting Foster over the hurdles, why notify the police? That was queer—and it wiped the grin off Haddock's face and got him rubbing his chin.

Someone cut loose with the wise crack that Foster had a nightmare, telephoned, and chucked the key out the window. This looked good but blew up when he showed the key to the front door still on his key-ring. What's more, he had only one key—a worn bit of a trinket, while the one that dropped from the window was brand new.

Yet, someone had rung up Headquarters, and someone had chucked down the key from his window. When you got down to hard tacks, you couldn't swear that Foster did either one of them. Lahley said the voice on the phone was weak and frightened—the figure at the window was indistinct.

When Lahley suggested that Foster must have forgotten to bolt the bed-room door, the Big Boss nearly had a stroke, he was so mad—and I sure had heard that heavy bolt slip back when he opened it.

Of course I was suspicious of Haddock. He sure had trotted in sudden on the party—but he was passing the house and saw a copper by the gate. If that proved true, you couldn't connect him up with it. As for Foster—I think he was just a bit suspicious of all of us. Trying to make him think we were on the job—all for his interest—mostly he talked about losing his sleep and the trying day

SAY IT WITH LEAD!

he would have tomorrow. I guess I was the only one who got the meaning of that—Sticker Haddock was to get the gate.

Boy! we searched that house while Foster paced the room—and cursed the outfit. Not a thing—not a sound—but the old place had more dark holes than Heinz has beans. And not a bottle—Foster was a slick old duck—the house was dryer than an anti-saloon league tract.

Of two things I was certain—someone had telephoned and someone had chucked down a key. Why a crook would want to advertise his presence I don't know. If a killer, why he didn't knock over Foster was another sticker. But I told Foster that I'd sit up with him—stay outside of his bed-room door the rest of the night. At first he couldn't see it at all, then came over and whispered to me.

"You must have your sleep—tomorrow night I may need you."

But he wouldn't let me stay there.

When Lahley and I both got at him—and Haddock too—he finally consented to let a copper lay guard outside his door—sit there in the den. When things were all set for a get-away, Haddock suggested another look over the house. If someone had telephoned and someone had thrown down the key, then someone was still in that house. The house was surrounded by cops and nobody could get out. Good enough! We started in to make the search again. But Foster sniffed—bawled Lahley out again for disturbing him.

"I need my sleep," he snapped angrily. "If you want to play hide and seek in my house all right, but don't disturb me again. If you find anyone, lock him up—I'll see him in the morning."

And turning into his room he slammed the door behind him. Bang went that bolt—Foster had some temper.

Another search was in order. I helped make a good job of it.

We didn't do much loud talking when we returned, unsuccessful, to the den. Tom Mooney was the harnessed bull left on guard—a superstitious lad who had done nothing but mutter, "Glory be to God" all the time he was in that house. But he was as big as an ox and certainly wouldn't fall asleep. Not he—his eyes kept getting wider and wider as he realized the mystery of the whole thing. But he drew his gun, and placing it across his knees, sat down before that thick oaken door which led to Foster's bed-room. A barred door—heavy bars before the window—a copper with a drawn gun watching, and things looked pretty good.

Even Haddock traveled in some fear of Howel L. Foster. At least, I was the only one who didn't tip-toe from that room. The great clock struck one as we filed out the front door. Haddock drove away first in a big touring car—and leaving the cops on the grounds to hoof it, Lahley, one policeman, and I jarred off in the Ford.

Back at the Police Station, Lahley spread himself for wind. But I didn't listen much. Somehow, I believed Foster's story—there didn't seem any sense in his lying to us. But—and a big BUT—why did someone wish to advertise his presence in the Foster household? That was a real crossworder and no mistake. As Foster said, I needed my sleep but I didn't want to take it in a chair, listening to the bed-time stories of the Chief—so I cut for it and trotted back to the hotel. If I had my way, we'd've had a shadow on Haddock—but I couldn't act there—Foster was keeping his knowledge about that bird under his hat.

No trap doors, no secret passages, no way to enter Foster's room and yet—but I was paid to protect Foster, not to solve crossword puzzles. So I slept—the real danger wasn't to come until Haddock got the air.

I was up early, did three eggs and a couple of chops, and strolled toward Foster's. No hurry, but I wanted to be on the job—this was the big day and Foster might feel nervous and want to get it over with early. Early or late—what's the difference? If it came to gun-play, Foster sure was there with the political pull. I whistled softly as I strolled along—eight-thirty.

Came the toot of a horn, the grinding of brakes, and a car swung up beside me.

"Hop in quick—it's Foster—killed sometime since we left."

Though there was a cool breeze in the morning air, I could plain-ly see the little beads of sweat dripping from Chief Lahley's forehead.

I clenched my fingers tightly as I jumped on the running board and slipped into the back. Foster dead! Surprised? Yes, I guess I was. Of course there was no loss to me—rather gain, when that will came to light, but—oh—there's a professional pride that goes before money. Why hadn't he let me sit outside that door?

"That mutt at the door—Tom Mooney—what of him?" I gulped.

"Don't know—just got the call—they broke in the door."

"They?" I sat up straighter.

"Haddock and Mooney—Haddock just got there—comes every morning to take Foster out to breakfast."

That was news—I whistled softly. If the body was still warm, I'd hang a bit of crepe over Haddock's ear and cash in on two hundred thousand dollars.

I didn't talk any more—just watched the white face of Lahley, and tried to do a bit of thinking. Lahley was shocked, certainly, and yet he knew of Foster's activities and must have expected just such a thing any time. Bootleggers have a way of being murdered.

Howel L. Foster was dead all right—there he lay stretched out on the floor by the side of the bed—that stern, cold look still marked him in death—those great sunken eyes now glared lifelessly out of the hollows. An ice-pick had done the trick—his own ice-pick—the one servant later identified it—stuck right through his heart. I had noticed it the night before—a needle-pointed thing with a nickel handle. Foster had kept it in his study to break ice for highballs.

Not a pretty sight, but during the excitement I did my stuff and got a good look around that room—the bolt too—broken by the blows of an axe as Mooney and Haddock pounded in the door. One glance at the body and Mooney had dashed downstairs to the phone.

I eyed Haddock pretty hard. Quick thoughts shot through my mind. If Haddock hadn't killed him, he should have—did he suspect how much of the truth about him Foster knew? Probably. Haddock read suspicion in my eyes and walking over to me, grinned.

"You'll have to do some thinking now—Mr. Gunman," he whispered. "Not in your line that—shooting men in the back is better, eh?"

Either sure of himself, or he hadn't done it! But I smiled easily and gave him a jolt.

"Better not turn your back then!" I was as cool as he.

He started slightly and straightened them broad, bent shoulders of his.

"You're through now." His mean little eyes were just two slits. "The meal ticket has gone out."

"Through?" My hand was just as near my hip pocket as his was. "No—only beginning."

He didn't get it and his face showed it. Twice he started to speak and stopped himself—the third time he just stopped anyway. The coroner, Doctor Fredricks, had come running up the stairs.

I didn't get all he said, for I was keeping an eye on Haddock. But I did hear him say that Foster had been dead at least six hours. The body found at eight—sometime between one and two—and the great clock had struck one when we had left the house. The murderer had little respect for the law then—or for me either—but then he hadn't heard about the will. But I shrugged my shoulders. Haddock had to be the boy—and yet—but we'd see what came of a few questions to Tom Mooney.

I couldn't walk around holding Haddock's hand—and I couldn't just accuse him of the murder. He had pull of his own—a certain fear he inspired anyway. As the confidential man of Foster's, he knew just what politicians were coming in for loose change. So I trot back to the police station with Chief Lahley, leaving Haddock at the house to take charge of things. Yep, that was his job. Funny! But after all he was the man closest to Foster—just the touch of comedy always found in tragedy. Ever notice it?

It was apparent from the start that Chief Lahley wasn't set on finding out too much. The way he went about questioning Tom Mooney was a joke—he glared at me a bit when I butted in—still he didn't have much guts and I got away with it.

Chapter 4

But Mooney wouldn't admit he was lying, and somehow I thought even the third degree would keep the story the same. But I did want him to admit that he fell asleep—that would help some. It was impossible to believe that he was in league with the murderer—let the killer call Foster to the door and watched him stabbed with the icepick. That was the logical conclusion of course. I couldn't see it any other way. But Mooney was so thick he was honest. The part of his story that I made him go over and over went like this.

"I sit there, you see—never once making a move—never leaving the room, you see. And morning comes, and I get up and pull up the shade—see—the sun comes in—see. At ten minutes of eight along comes Haddock."

"How did he get in the front door?" I ask, sudden-like.

"Why, I let him in—see."

"And you didn't leave the room—see, see." I chucked some of them loose "sees" at him, but I couldn't shake him.

"Haddock and me go upstairs, see—then he knocks at the door—then he turns to me and knocks again. No answer, see. He sends me down in the cellar for an axe. I get it, see, and I takes it and busts down the door—one look—and I fall back—see. Foster is lying there, the ice-pick sticking from his chest—see. Then I run to the phone."

I try to get him to can the "sees" and do, a little. But he was sure Foster was dead. Haddock is alone with him for five minutes, maybe—no more. That much I find out. But it don't do any good. Mooney is a witness to the ice-pick in Foster's chest; the coroner said that Foster had been dead at least six hours—nothing to go on there. And that's that. Mooney is a thick hick but he sticks to his story and—impossible maybe—but somehow I believe him. He's willing to help me all he can.

Chief Lahley is in a pretty state. Besides being a big boss, Foster is his friend—but to delve too deeply into the murder is apt to bring some very unpleasant things to light. I dare say the dear old chief had troubles of his own.

Then he chirps suddenly.

"I wonder if Haddock will notify his wife—or is that my duty?" He half reaches for the phone and hesitates.

"What wife—whose?"

This case is sure full of surprises.

"Foster's, of course—I thought you knew."

And I didn't. He had never mentioned her to me. Still—I got my breath.

"Where is she?" I asked.

But he shook his head as he lifted the receiver.

"Some mountain hotel. Haddock will know," he said, as he gave the number of the Foster residence.

Haddock knew a lot and no mistake. And now the man whom Foster feared above all others was taking charge of things up at the house. Where was the lawyer? I put that question and a dozen others to Lahley, but the best I got was: "Haddock will know."

That was enough for me—Lahley was like a balloon: besides being full of gas he was no earthly good. So I walked out and left him flat. I'd have to play a lone hand.

I never did have any use for private detectives, but it looked like I'd have to be one myself. I start out by tracing up Haddock—just what he did when he left us the night before. And he left a trail that a blind man could follow. Went straight in his car over to the town of Hillsbury twenty miles away, arriving there at one-forty-five a.m. and he spent the night—you'd never guess it—in jail. Got himself pinched for speeding. Turned sulky and wouldn't identify himself that night. But the next morning at six-thirty he got loud—spoke of his friend, Foster, and demanded to see the Chief of the Hillsbury police at once. Foster's name worked there too; the Chief trotted down, knew Haddock, and turned him loose. That was at seven-fifteen. From there he came straight to Middlend.

Checking up the time, you couldn't hang the crime on him. Hot stuff, that! Some alibi but—a planned alibi. Haddock must have known that something was going to happen and wanted to be able to show a clean pair of hands. Why should he be suspected? There was only one answer—he knew of Foster's suspicions and my purpose in town. He might even have thought that Foster was going to railroad him back to prison. With that alibi goes my two hundred thousand dollars for blowing off Haddock. If that little affair took place now, it would have to come under the head of pleasure. Haddock couldn't very well have committed that murder. He was a shrewd duck, but that planted alibi was bad stuff. It let me know for certain that he had a hand in the killing some place.

I'll be frank about it—I was dead set on running down that murderer. The will said two hundred thousand dollars for bringing the right man to justice—and—well, the bird who killed Foster wasn't the kind who gets taken alive. I could use two hundred thousand berries—none better.

Of course I wanted to take another slant around that house. For a moment I was beginning to take real seriously to those fairy stories about secret passages. Foster was bolted in—it was a cinch that no one hurled that ice-pick through the window at him. And there was thought there; if he hadn't been lying in such a position to make such a stunt impossible, I'd almost believe it—but the bars were too narrow. And I come up sharp, with a start. Not a thinker, eh? Man! I had a thought then that would've made Sherlock Holmes look cheap. Bars at the window—get it—that's me, Kid.

I slip up to Foster's house, bent on meeting the wife while she's in the first shock of her sorrow. Just want to see how really bad she does feel—and Haddock meets me at the door. Meets me and leaves me. Just opens the door—chirps out an old line.

"Don't think you own the house because you stepped on the welcome mat," he says, with that ugly sneer. "You're fired—beat it."

And I was standing outside. Just one strange sound had come from within—the soft sob of a woman. Now what? I turn and beat it straight to Lahley—can't very well force myself into the house of the dead—besides—well, Haddock must be acting for the widow— that sob was right behind him in the hall. Unless she was deaf, she had gathered in his cheap wit.

Lahley hears my weep like a stepfather listening to the wails of a heavily insured step-son. Not that he don't want to help, maybe, but he has more stalls than a livery stable.

"I must protect myself first, Williams," he says, "and honestly I can't see where you fit. Mrs. Foster is the boss and Haddock's her friend."

And I wondered how much of a friend—or more. But in that house I'll have to get; so I trot over to Foster's lawyer, Arthur Marston. I've decided to weep on his shoulder if necessary.

This Marston is so honest he wouldn't skin a banana—he tells me so himself, and he looks shrewdly at me and pushes in his turned up button of a nose—funny way he has of doing it, too—looks almost like a deliberate insult, but it ain't.

"There's the police." He brings his pompous little body to his feet and runs it across the room. "It's their business, you know— they'll no doubt be running all over the house, Mr. Williams. Mrs. Foster will have enough to bother about—and I have no authority to use the estate's money hiring private—er—confidential agents." He takes another squint at my card.

"But I don't want any pay—I just want to solve the mystery."

"Ah—a philanthropic detective—most laudable—but—" His shrewd little eyes regarded me steadily.

I winked broadly—this mouth-piece was no hick, so I give him the news.

"You see, I've been paid enough to go on for a while—and—" I paused a minute to let him get the full meaning, "I know about the will—that clause—the two hundred thousand berries."

He turned around quick enough at that. He didn't think I knew—

hoped I didn't. Why? But he thought quickly, did little Arthur.

"Foster was my friend." He comes over and plants his five feet two before me. "Perhaps, Mr. Williams, I might personally hire you to clear up this mystery."

"And I'll sign a paper about that money, eh?"

"I'll help you—and we'll split it." He didn't wait long for his dirt and his eyes shone with greed. "I'll be a lot of help," he added, as I got up and started for the door. Too many papers handy, and when you get to writing your name for a wise lawyer you're signing away your soul.

I know it was bad policy to irritate him—but I couldn't help it. He was so cheap—he was a bargain. But he had me by the arm before I reached the door.

"It's not exactly in the will," he whispers softly in my ear. "That would take time—it's a trust fund already created and payable at once. I can help—I—"

I made an enemy all right, but what's the difference? I never split. Like as not this lad would try to hang the crime on half a dozen, and I'd be the goat—shooting up the town.

"You'll be sorry." He follows me to the door, and there's a threat in his voice now. "I could have had you made a deputy sheriff—then you'd do your shooting legally—now—if you get the money—you'll be in jail."

There was some sense in that, I thought, as I shot down the elevator. If Lahley would only—but what's the use—Lahley had the backbone of an oyster—and perhaps I'm flattering Lahley.

Chapter 5

I stepped out of an elevator and brought up dead. Bing—like that— I'd walked into a Central Office man from the city. Silent Conners— the sharpest dick on the force. What was he doing in Middlend— and what was he doing in that building? He just nodded and smiled—we didn't speak—dicks and I have nothing in common.

That he was going to see Arthur Marston was certain—three minutes later a buck slipped to the elevator boy certified that little thought. More against me now—it was a cinch that this Silent Conners was doing a split with the mouth-piece. What a double-crossing little runt he was; no doubt he was splitting with Haddock and a few more.

Central Office men are not easily shipped this far north; so I put through a long distance call to New York and got in touch with Inspector Crowley, who's a white guy and a good friend of mine. Silent Conners had got a leave of absence. I don't know, but I felt sort of mad—somehow it was as if they were trying to steal my money. And yet—that trust fund had been made before I was consulted—two hundred grand—yep, I'd grab it despite them all. If "he travels fastest who travels alone" was going to work out, why—I was as friendless as any ten, twenty and thirty orphan ever hoped to be. And if I did draw a bead on the murderer—blooey—the big house for mine—half the town would be working for my hide. Well—oh, to hell with them! That's the way I felt.

Trotting around town, I heard some things. Mrs. Foster had been married about five years—she was young too—hardly more than twenty-seven. She had been out driving with Haddock a few times certainly. Where had she been? Up at one of her husband's hotels in the Adirondacks—he owned several—not generally known perhaps. And that was that. Lahley steered clear of me, like I was the plague, and I knew the cause of that. Marston and Haddock had both visited him at the Police Station.

I was an outcast—just one apparent friend—the star reporter for the rival paper, who hated Foster and his politics like poison. He smelled trouble, and tried to get something out of me. If it had of been one of the big dailies, I could have pulled down a pretty pile—but five hundred dollars would have been a fortune to these hicks.

They hustled through the inquest and the funeral. And they couldn't keep me out of the house then. I was a witness, and I pulled my story. Nothing to hide—just the truth from me. Foster had feared death and hired me. I said nothing about Haddock—when that portion of the will got out—well—you know what you'd do for two hundred thousand dollars.

I could fill a book with the questions that were asked—nothing ever mentioned about liquor, mind you—oh, no—nice, clean little inquest and the jury pondered and thought and ate a few hundred sandwiches, and then brought in the remarkable verdict that Foster had met his death at the hands of some person or persons unknown. They agreed that the ice-pick was the weapon. The wisdom of a dozen Solomons sure did come off there. And Haddock was questioned, like the gentleman that he ain't.

108

One thing more only—Tom Mooney told the same story—
almost word for word. And he wasn't in uniform either—which
may or may not have been all right—but Lahley treated him like
dirt—pretty poor dirt, too. Lahley avoided looking at me, but as far
as I was concerned, he could go peg mud at himself. He had something to be nervous about—already the rival paper was putting him
over the jumps—what with Foster being killed while the whole
police force was guarding the house.

As yet they didn't razz me—but they would. Just laying off in
hopes I'd give them a little information. It was a live sheet and no
mistake.

I hung around the house just as long as I could after the inquest.
Haddock was continually whispering to the heavily veiled Mrs.
Foster. Silent Conners, from the city, apparently slept in a big
chair—at least, his eyes were closed and there was a cherub-like
smile on his face. If I wanted to beat this bird I'd have to work fast.
My stuff is action—his, deduction—you can see the jump he had on
me in this case. Point out the man, and I'd beat him to the draw any
time.

Marston, the mouth-piece, was edging around toward me, to
give me the office to beat it, but I took the jump on him—slipped
out into the hall—opened and banged the front door, and dashed up
the stairs. Did anyone see me? Had Tom Mooney caught a glimpse
of me there as he came out into the hall? I could hear Marston's
voice below, shrilly asking: "Has that cheap gunman from the city
gone out this way?"

And Tom Mooney's answer cheered me considerably.

"Just went out the door," he said. "And, Mr. Marston—I wish
you'd speak to the Chief—it's a terrible disgrace to be put off the
force like this—an incompetent in my own home town—why,
people even look on me with suspicion."

I heard no more—any moment they might find me—I wanted
another look in that bed-room. And I got it. All the time I wanted—
no one had a thought for me. Here's my verdict and I'll stick to it: If
there were any traps or secret passages to that room I'll eat my hat
at the end of this yarn—and remember, I was wearing a good sized
slouch hat. But it goes just the same.

The bars at the window again—closely formed, strong, round
bits of iron they were—I pulled each one separately.

Then I watched the machines slipping from the house. A sad picture, I suppose. Things were moving fast—the house was deserted. They were planting Foster. But I raised my hat as the procession turned out the gate—no big display—the King was dead.

I'd have liked to get a crack at Foster's papers but no chance of that—they must have been put away in the big safe I had seen in the library downstairs. The study desk was open—everything cleaned out of it. No time wasted in a politician's affairs. Lahley had no guts—everything should have been sealed up—then—oh—I'd have broken the seals.

They sure got rid of Foster fast—in less than an hour I heard a car at the door—a feminine voice—then the deeper tones of Haddock. He was back with the widow. Was I caught? I shrugged my shoulders—they daren't do more than put me out. How much I knew, Haddock couldn't tell. Of course, if he wanted gun-play—well—another coroner's inquest would give the town something to talk about, and I felt that I'd be the star witness—not Haddock.

They didn't come upstairs but went straight to the library, and I could hear their voices murmuring—then raised in hot debate. Friends of course—but things were not so good. When thieves fall out, so to speak. So I just sneaked down those stairs—and planted myself close to the library door.

"I can't. I won't. I don't believe it." Fear and passion both were in the woman's voice.

"It's not for you to judge—but a jury." A pause and I could almost hear Haddock smack his lips. "Besides—there's the other way and two hundred thousand dollars—not as much as the fortune you got, of course—but a pile of jack."

"You never, never—dared talk like this to me before." The woman again—but more of pleading than anger in her voice.

"I never had such a hold on you—before." And Haddock's voice was smooth as ice—and just about as cold too. Then his voice trailed off so low I couldn't get it.

Flat against that keyhole I pushed my ear. There was the slightest stop to my heart. Had the woman done it? Did Haddock know? And— Great God! I couldn't force a confession out of a woman— two hundred thousand dollars and—

Haddock's voice raised in anger.

"No, you don't—you damned little slut." A shuffle—a scream—

Chapter 6

I just burst open that door and stepped into the room. A dark-haired woman was on her knees at Haddock's feet—her body half twisted around—her face screwed up in agony as Haddock held her wrist—her arm twisted above her shoulder.

A common thug, Haddock—perhaps—but in that brief moment I had a certain respect for him. Quick—man, I never saw anything like it. He was shoving something into his pocket with his left hand—and unnoticed from that pocket had fluttered a tiny bit of paper—right by my foot, then under it—but without seeing just where it came from I was looking down the muzzle of his great black automatic—and—well, of course my forty-four was tickling his chin. For a bit, it looked like the coroner of this town is going to earn his salary.

It's Haddock who breaks the strain as the woman comes to her feet. He just laughs—lets that long narrow mouth of his slip over toward his ears.

"It's our little gunman," he says contemptuously, but I see that his eyes never leave my gat. "Hiding under a bed again, I dare say. And now what?"

I only get a half glance at the woman—pretty, in a sad sort of way—looks like her life wasn't all roses—even if she did marry money—those sad eyes had dirty money written in every deep line beneath them.

I spoke slowly.

"He has something of yours that you want?"

How I was going to get whatever it was I don't know.

For the first time, Haddock's eyes left my gun—just a flash of warning to the woman. She got it and wilted.

"Nothing—no, nothing. You have no right in my house—you had better go—go now."

It was like a school piece, the way it came out, and her eyes were on Haddock—her thin, delicate chest rising and falling rapidly. She feared this man—like a frightened animal she was.

"Drop your gun," Haddock said, "and get out."

But I couldn't see it that way. Here was a good chance for him to shoot. He had the woman scared enough to lie that he did his killing in self-defense. So, being a cautious man, I held my gun steady. I

111

could see Haddock weighing the problem carefully in his mind. He knew my reputation as well as I knew his. But he had me wrong—I'm no murderer. Still he held onto his gun. As for me, I was willing to go, but I wanted that bit of paper under my foot. But neither one of us would lower a gun and there you have it. Mine was the tougher job—Haddock was signaling the woman with his eyes—and she was shifting around behind me. Not so good that, but I daren't turn and watch her. So I warned him.

"The minute a hand touches me—you die, Haddock." And I meant it.

When it looked like the nervous strain of waiting would get too much for one of us, and a trigger would just naturally be pulled, the doorbell rang. The servant answered it, and Tom Mooney was in the room.

And that's that. It worked like magic. With a witness like Mooney we both felt safe—our guns just slipped away—funny thing that.

Haddock sneered and turned to the telephone—the woman just dashed from the room and I heard her feet upon the stairs. And I—I just ducked down, grabbed that bit of paper and stepped out the door as I heard Haddock chirping:

"Police Station—Chief Lahley—Haddock talking."

Tom Mooney followed me down the steps like a faithful servant. I hadn't wanted an audience, but Tom had sure come at the right time. And he had his troubles—fired from the force. He had seen me sneak upstairs at the time he told Marston I had gone out. He knew the town was against me—but so were they against him. I had treated him fair—believed him, he thought, and now—he wanted to help—anything to find the murderer and re-establish himself in the eyes of his neighbors.

Then I got my idea—he was a cop—must know something of the graft. By Jove—here was an opportunity. I jerked Mooney up a side street and pumped him dry.

There they found us. Two big coppers—stuttering slightly as they gave me the sad news.

"You're wanted around at Headquarters," the big bull chirped, like they had more than one Station House. "Chief Lahley wants to see you."

"And if I won't come?" I looked right in his eyes.

"Then—we're to drag you there."

Both of them half felt for their clubs or guns or both maybe. But I laughed.

"You'd look pretty dragging me there. I'll go with you." I turned to Mooney, who stood at my side, his huge fists clenched tightly. "Meet me at the hotel at seven tonight, Tom," I said, good-naturedly.

Then I walked down the street between the two comedy cops.

"I wouldn't make any dates, young feller." One of them tried to be a regular New York cop. "You won't see no one tonight—not you."

I smiled and shrugged my shoulders. My talk with Mooney had been a good one. I'd sure jar up the dear old Chief. He'd drag me in like a common crook, would he?

"Williams," Lahley shoved his cigar from one side of his mouth to the other, as we sat alone in his private room; "I should lock you up—and could—housebreaking is a serious charge. But I'm going to let you go. There's the six-ten train—take it to New York, and I'll forget the charge—but you must pass your word not to come back again."

I only smiled at him. After all, poor Lahley wasn't such a bad bird. They had his number, that was all. He feared the political power of Marston—and whoever else was behind that rum running game.

I didn't stall—I chirped right out what was on my chest. Gave him facts and figures of how much graft he had received and how some of it was paid. Tom Mooney might have been thick, but he sure had powers of observation. And Lahley turned as red as an overripe tomato.

"No vague fears, mine, Chief," I told him as I flipped open a box and lit up one of his choice cigars. "I'm talking turkey now—one chirp out of you and all I know goes to the *Daily Star.* Come—"

I placed a hand on his shoulder. Wilted—he was indeed an old man—just a pawn in the game.

"For all your tinsel and buttons and shining gold seal, you're only playing at being a Police Chief," I told him. "Stick to me and I'll fix you. There's two hundred thousand dollars in it—I won't be stingy—I'll slip you five thousand berries if you're a good kid—if you ain't—blooey!" I snapped my fingers. "The *Daily Star* and I will make a real monkey out of you—and a crooked one, too."

"I'd help if I could." He sort of leaned wearily on the desk. "Secretly, I will—" he looked up hopefully, "—but I couldn't take money for it—no—not money. I was a friend of Foster—what—what'll I tell the others, though? And what do you want me to do?"

He was coming around right; so I shot the load off my chest.

"Tell them pressure was brought to bear higher up—that you'll pretend to work with me and keep me in the dark. Then make me a deputy sheriff."

"I'll do it," he finally blurted out.

He was between the devil and the deep blue sea and I was both of them. I didn't waste time. In less than an hour I had a nice little badge which gave me the privilege of doing my killing—if need be—legally. And he told me, too, that Silent Conners had also been sworn in as a deputy. Good enough. Marston had given me the idea.

"Another thing." I stuck a finger into his stomach at parting. "To stop the *Daily Star* panning you, you'd better offer a reward—get the mayor and make it snappy—a good round sum for the capture dead or alive of the murderer of Howel L. Foster."

"Dead or alive," he muttered. "Dead—I'll do it. And, Mr. Williams—I'll be a great help to you—five thousand isn't much money—not when you think of two hundred thousand."

"Make it ten." I patted him on the back. "I'll give you ten if everything comes off as advertised."

Funny bird, old Lahley—likable bit of a grafter at that. The old-time song "Everybody's Doing It" just slipped out as I hummed my way through the surprised faces of those moving picture policemen.

Not so bad. Here was a bit of business requiring brains. Not my line, you say—well, my line was out and I was fishing for Haddock.

Back in the hotel I examined that bit of paper I'd picked from the floor—a torn bottom of a letter, I took it. No telling whom it was to—hardly Haddock, for the ending was in a clear, round hand: Your loving Edgar.

That was my job then—to find this loving Edgar. If he had put his last name to it! But I suppose it's these little things that make life interesting. Twice I tried to write the whole thing out, point by point—that a, b, c stuff of all good detectives, but that only made matters worse—the thing was to find Edgar. Nothing special in mind when I slipped out on Main Street—just sparring for time—

giving the cops a chance to see me still breezing around town.

And I spot Silent Conners—just get a glimpse of him slipping out of a jewelry store. Farrington & Son is smeared across the front of it. He don't see me—at least, he don't look at me. For a second I think of shadowing him—take a step forward and stop. Silly, that— Conners has more eyes than a potato. His coming out of the jewelry store don't mean much or—Gad! I slip back behind a telegraph pole. Farrington & Son is picking up in business—that is, if they ain't particular about their customers—Sticker Haddock had just passed through the big front doors.

He never gave a look to left or right. I'm eager to see what he's buying in there. So far, things have been as dull as ten p.m. in Philadelphia. I step off the curb and start across the street.

And start is right—only for a telegraph pole and a post box just behind me on the curb, it would be good-night for Race Williams. A car shoots down—swerves across the street and squeezes in on me. I make the curb, but so does the car—it's getting between the two poles that saves me. Sudden! Man—it missed me by— Oh, less than that.

I didn't get the license number—it had been too carefully caked with mud for that, but I looked straight into a sinister, evil face as the car sped by. Though his cap was pulled well down, one thing marked him for sure identification—one eye had looked at me—the other right on down the road—get it? This duck was sporting a glass eye, and what's more he'd need a mate to it if he ever crossed my path again.

Now, I do my watching in safety. There's a little coupé across, just down the street—so I climb in that and watch the store. Haddock and another fellow come out—a youngish, delicate sort of chap, with a quick, nervous walk and a head that spins around like a top. This lad is no hard-boiled crook—crooks, like dog-catchers, are born—not made. But his conscience isn't easy, or he wouldn't keep doing the whirling dervish act. Up the street they argue, and I nearly fall out of the coupé—then the lad turns back and Haddock peddles along alone.

That's my cue. If this bird is in the game, he'll soon have me pointed out to him—before he does, I'll act. I've got a hunch who the nervous youth is, but where he fits—

I'm right on his heels, and he hardly gets his hat off and slips behind the counter before I brace him. He's the son, I take it—the only other occupant is an oldish gent. I just pick up one of their business cards and scratch hurriedly on it.

"Want you to fix up my watch—sort of sentimental about it— must have a receipt."

He smiled slightly—relieved too, I thought.

"We always give a receipt," he says loftily.

Yep—a stamped and numbered one. But aloud:

"This will suit me—just go over the watch—I'll come in to see what you found wrong with it tomorrow."

He takes the card briskly enough, swings it around—spots "Race Williams" and near drops it. So he's been told about me. But he don't get a chance to recover.

"Sign the receipt," I snap. "There."

I slip my fountain pen into his twitching fingers. He's flustered but he signs, and I'm out the door.

"Edgar Farrington" is on that card in a fine round hand. The (E) and the (g) in Edgar have a most familiar twist.

I whistle softly—some detective—eh, what?

Chapter 7

That night Tom Mooney and I play the regular stuff, and watch the Foster house. Not a servant there yet—Haddock has been seen in town, and I'm waiting to see if little Edgar trots around. I'm getting mighty impatient and no mistake. With Silent Conners, the best dick that ever framed an innocent man, on the job, I'll have to work fast. Little Edgar don't show up; but at nine o'clock Mrs. Foster slips out, hops a car waiting at the curb beyond the gate and flashes toward town. Good enough—I put my little scheme to the test.

I'm setting the stage for a return engagement of that night we boys thought we saw Foster throw the key down from the window. Imagination is all right, but I like to see events acted out.

It's a treat to watch Tom Mooney's face when I jimmy the kitchen window in the back—one minute—two—and we're inside.

"Tom," I said; "I'll repeat my instruction. We won't have a whole lot of time, and I want the thing pulled off right the first crack."

He's a good boy is Tom, listens and repeats what I tell him. Then I drop back on the lawn. There couldn't have been a better night for it—conditions are just about the same as the night the key came from that barred bed-room window of Howard L. Foster. In a few minutes we'll know just what sort of a deep thinking dick Race Williams is. With that I trot around to the front of the house and take my position just beneath that barred window.

I'm careful too—stand just where I did the other night. Two windows are plainly visible—not too clear you understand—mistily they stand forth against the shadows of the stone, the overhanging eaves above Foster's window and the thick vines that cling to the heavy walls.

There's a creak of a raising window and the dull outline of a shadow there in the window of the study next to the bed-room. Tom calls softly down to me, and I call softly back,

"Chuck down your coat and hat."

I give him the office, then watch them fall on the grass beside me.

There's a change at once—his white shirt is clear, now, standing out ghostlike against the blackness of the huge stone structure. Tom climbs out the study window—steps on the ledge and moves cautiously along. Funny he looks—just his head and white shirt visible. His legs too if you watch closely when he moves, otherwise it looks like a head and trunk were moving—gliding along that wall.

Pretty soon he gets right in front of Foster's window, and stops dead. The effect is good—makes me gasp—you'd actually think he was inside the room and that the lower casement of the window hid his feet. He's a good actor is Tom—goes through all the motions of tossing down a key.

But the one thing stands out now—the thing I'm looking for— the thing I'd thought over until I almost busted my think-box. There are bars on that window, and yet, thinking it over afterward, I had a distinct impression that no bars had stood out on the white shirt of the man who had stood in that window a few nights before. I snap my fingers. No bars across the shirt that other night—none now. The man who tossed down that key *had not been in the room at all* but had stood on the ledge in front of the window just as Tom Mooney did now.

I ain't satisfied though. I'm going to do the thing thorough. Yep, I make Tom duck behind those vines—toss up his coat to him and have him slip it on. Man, he just fades from view there. The bird who threw the key that night had simply stood on the ledge, concealed in the heavy vines, while we searched the house from cellar to attic. Watching his chance, he had climbed down from the ledge when the search was over—and slipped away! Simple!

So much for that. Then I call up to him. This time he slips through the study window and into Foster's room and looks down at me from inside. Nothing to it—of course I'm right. His white shirt is visible from inside—not so clear as outside though, and besides the bars streak right down him and across too.

Of a certainty the man who threw down that key was not in the room at all. But why did he do it? That's the ticket—why telephone the police of his presence in the house? Damn it—the truth only made things worse. I wasn't getting any nearer to solving the mystery—and I was becoming as busy as a two headed cat in a fish store. Once again I drag Tom out on the ledge. But the thing's settled—it's the same picture over again as that of the other night— the murder night.

Mrs. Foster is back—the car swinging straight in the gate this time. I whistle softly to Mooney, who hides behind the vines—then I plant myself close against the wall. Haddock is with her—and they're fighting again. Lovers' quarrels, I wonder. As they pass in, Tom climbs to the ground and we beat it to town.

One more chance at detecting. I'll brace little Edgar. He must know something. I'll take a chance—accuse him of being on the ledge—find out just where he was the night of the murder and—

Determinedly Mooney and I trot along. He knows Edgar's hangout—above the jewelry store—some altercation with his father, Mooney thinks; though the town has it he sleeps there to protect the store.

Another jolt and a real one. Right in Edgar's doorway I bump into Silent Conners. And this time he speaks—mean, sneaking little speech that he thinks funny.

"Ah—" he raises those eyebrows of his, "—Mary's little lamb again."

With that, he's gone. I wonder if he really thinks I've been following him around. But at that I've got to admit he's a trick ahead of me—beat me to the jewelry store too. Clever duck.

Edgar Farrington is in—and from his face I can see he's ripe to pull over the coals. Guess Silent Conners has pumped him dry.

"You—you too," he mutters, throwing himself on the bed and

burying his head in his hands. "Whom do you suspect—what now—I know nothing—I saw nothing—I won't say a word more—I've said too much already—I—"

I intended to be clever—force the truth by well-directed questions—play at being a detective, but I suddenly changed my mind. It wasn't my game—I was through—I wanted action—wanted the truth and I knew how to get it.

"Get outside," I said to Tom Mooney. "Guard that door—and not a word, no matter what you hear." With Tom outside, I turn to Edgar.

"You won't talk, eh?" I step close to him and jerk up his head. "If you don't open up that head of yours I'll open it for you and see what your brains contain."

Tough on the kid perhaps, but then, one can't make catsup without smashing a few tomatoes.

"She didn't do it—didn't do it." He starts in to turn on the weeps.

A new idea struck me at once. He thought I knew as much as Conners—maybe I did. But I changed my tune a bit.

"If you don't open up with all you know in one minute—I'll arrest her for murder. You looked through the window and saw it."

That last was purely a wild guess. A good one? Yes and no. It was wrong, of course, but it brought him straight up—wildly denying my chance shot.

"Listen, Kid." I saw he was ripe to unload. "I don't believe she did, either." And for a moment I didn't. I wasn't positive who the "she" was. Another guess—"What were you doing on that ledge—what did you throw down that key for?"

"Yes," he nods, "the detective from the city knew that. Oh—why won't Ethel come to me?"

And now the cat was out—Ethel was Mrs. Foster. Here was "loving Edgar"—and he had been making a saucy story out of a perfectly good bootlegger scheme. So I led him on—wouldn't have to muss up the place with him after all.

"I'm your friend." I lied easily. "Don't trust—Haddock."

"Haddock—Haddock." He came wildly to his feet. "He says she did it—made me keep away from her and—Great God! I love her. No—tell them I did it—anything."

He sure was one wild baby. Slowly and surely he was spilling the dirt. One more lead and I had him.

"How about Haddock—?"

No more—I just got started.

"Yes—yes—Haddock—he—but how could he do it?"

"How?" I gasp. "Don't you know—didn't you look through the window?"

Tough—I thought for a moment that the whole secret was out. A clasp on his shoulder—the promise that I was his friend and would help him and the woman—and—he came through clean. No threat there—just a bit of love. Ethel was playing around with Haddock. Bad that! I hadn't traced up her alibi yet—and again, maybe someone pulled the killing for her.

But here's Edgar's story and it rings true—strange but true.

He loved Ethel Foster, who had practically been forced into a rotten marriage with Foster through her father's politics. What she didn't know about her husband's crooked activities, she soon learned, and Edgar was willing to help her find it all out. He wanted her to get a divorce—skip out—anything—and dash through the clouds with him. It was a pretty story of moonlight rides and hidden supper parties. And of course Foster grew suspicious. Husband and wife had one grand row—Mrs. Foster demanding a divorce, and Foster locking her up in the house for a bit. "Me and the Boy Friends" didn't work so good with him.

She managed to slip a note out to Edgar, telling him of her fear of her husband. Then had come that last letter with the key. She was frightened—he must sneak up to the barred room and find her—if— And that's the way the pitiful little note ended. Edgar talked it over with his father—another row there. The police were useless because of Foster's political pull. Then, one day he missed her face at the barred window—and learned from the one servant that Mrs. Foster had gone off to a hotel in the mountains. He didn't believe it, but—

"I went up there—saw the manager of the hotel—he said she wasn't there."

The rest of it he spilled like this:

"Frantic, I came back to town. Foster had gone to New York—here was a chance to search the house. I was crazy, I guess, but I thought—oh, that he had killed her. I just got in the house, when Foster returned. I heard his feet slip over the boards without—the sudden twist of his key in the lock. I was frightened—ran into the kitchen and hid there. But Foster never searched the house—never even suspected my presence. He just tramped up the stairs through the little study to his bed-room. I heard the great bolt shoot home behind him.

"Now what—could I search the house with Foster in it. Part of it, yes—but not that bed-room—not that barred room in which Foster was. And if I found her what? Found her dead? I'd be accused of her murder. I had no right in the house. I—it was then that I thought of the telephone. A match that I struck flared up straight above the instrument. I couldn't get the police to search the house for me. Not with Foster's pull. But if they thought that Foster sent for them—called for help in the middle of the night like that. Surely they'd search the house then. If Foster forbade them to after a mysterious call in the night—ah, then, I'd have a story to tell—demand justice."

Edgar paused a moment—looked at me an instant—read the interest in my face—the belief too, I guess, and ran on—anxious to be done with it—get the load off his chest.

"I called the police—lowered my voice to a hoarse frightened whisper which was not hard for me to do then. Somehow in the background was ever the dead body—of Mrs. Foster. The call worked—I didn't say too much—couldn't—the words choked in my throat. The receiver fell back on the hook and the thought came. Suppose Foster didn't even let them in—sent them away while at his bed-room window. That was it—at his window—I ran up those steps—careful—cautious I guess, but ran just the same. The study door was partly opened—I slipped through—sought the window and climbed out on the ledge. I knew exactly what I wanted to do then—my brain worked clearly—my plan was perfect—all grown in my head in an instant.

"My feet never wavered—somehow, just the thought that I was doing it for her steadied me. And I came before the bars in Foster's bed-room window—stood there an instant—then slipped off my coat. So, crouched low, I waited—heard your car—saw it drive in— pull up before the house. It was then I acted—one hand held the black coat across my knees—the other waved to you and the police. I forget what I did—I was frightened—in deadly terror when I threw down the key. Enough—I did it. I put on my coat and concealed myself behind the vines when you all crowded into the vestibule, and waited until the search was over. Surely the police would search better than I could. No chance to hide Foster's crime, I thought—or if Ethel Foster was still alive they'd find her. Oh, I must have been crazy."

Crazy was right. True—I fired a couple of questions at him.

"Why don't you see her? Why—what makes you think she did the—killing?"

Because he did think so—you could see it in his eyes.

He hung his head a minute, then looked up.

"Haddock has been to see me—forbids my seeing her. He—oh, he wants her money—he don't love her. No one could love her like I do. I would swear to the killing."

But he didn't answer my second question.

"Kid," I said, "what is Haddock to you—why don't you go see her anyway?"

"She forbids it too." And his head went down again.

"That isn't all," I told him. "A real man don't let the woman he loves suffer alone—at a time like this."

"God! I can't go to her." He was up, pacing the room now. "If I do, Haddock will accuse her of murder."

"Then you think her guilty." I shot the words at him.

"No—no—I couldn't—it's—he'll accuse her."

"That wouldn't get him anywhere. The door was bolted on the inside. You can't hang the crime on anyone—no one could get in."

"He will lie—send her to the chair. Oh, he's devilish clever—listen." And he clutched me by the arm. "He will swear that the door was not bolted—that he only said that it was to shield her."

"Was it bolted?"

I come out fast—after all we only had Haddock's word for that. Tom Mooney was telephoning. Still—Haddock couldn't have done it. The man had been dead too long.

"Yes—but he'll say it wasn't—accuse her—I think that he will force her to marry him. She can't prove—where she was."

"And where was she—all this time you searched for her?"

He hesitated—then: "At the hotel in the Adirondacks. The one I wrote to. It was owned by Foster. The manager kept my letters to her, and hers to me. They would convince any jury of her hatred of her husband, and of her desire to be rid of him. Now—Haddock has them."

I knew that.

"But the night of the murder—where was she then?"

"That's the trouble." Edgar's face was very wan and drawn. "She had run away from the hotel—got lost in the woods and only found her way back to the hotel in the morning. She has no alibi."

"Like you," I said, pointedly.

"Like me? It was nearly four o'clock before I got a chance to drop from that ledge and slip by the policemen about the house. I don't care though—not for myself—I think Haddock will force her to marry him—she's very wealthy—now."

So the only one with an alibi was the one who should have done the killing—Haddock.

Chapter 8

I left Edgar, full of more thoughts—when was the action coming in? I was tired of thinking.

If that door wasn't bolted, you could hang the crime on either Edgar or the woman without much trouble. Both had motives—the letters would prove that. And Haddock had the letters. He couldn't have done it, and yet—Tom and I stepped from the door and the long expected action was ripe.

Just under a street light I saw the one-eyed driver who had tried to run me down. He was coming our way and was ten feet down the street. He saw me all right for he speeded up—too late.

"Come on, Tom," I cried—dashed out into the street—made a clutch—grabbed the car and swung safely aboard.

If he had a gun he didn't make a reach for it—pretended great surprise. But my gat, concealed in my overcoat pocket, held him as the car stopped and Tom Mooney lumbered up.

It was a misty, drizzly night and only one lad took in the little drama there on Main Street. Just one lad—but one was enough. Quietly watching us from under an awning that had not been raised, was Silent Conners. I lamped him good as we sped by. This was my trick—and I tipped my hat as we sped toward the Police Station.

And Conners—was he knocked cockeyed at my beating him to this lad? Not a chance—he bowed as he too raised his hat. A queer duck, Conners, and no mistake. But I noticed too that he followed slowly in the wake of the car. Good—he was taking my dust for a change.

This lad sure was one tough bird and mighty sure of himself, as he sneered evilly at me. But I sat beside him now—my gun in his ribs. I stopped him a block from the Police Station and sent Tom Mooney for the Chief. I wanted to get this rat in without a bunch of cops looking him over and squealing to someone higher up. Haddock was on my mind.

Chief Lahley hems and haws a bit, but we slip One-Eye through a side door and into a little cell. It's getting late and not many cops around—as for prisoners—there ain't none.

"You can't just lock me up like this." He slips the good eye on Lahley and leaves the marble one on me. "I want to see Haddock—I ain't done nothing—but there'll be an awful stink if you don't turn me loose."

"Gun-toting, is the charge," I call, loud enough for Lahley to hear as he stands outside the cell, rubbing his chin.

Then I pull a nice brace of gats and a knife out of One-Eye's pocket.

"I got a license for that."

He swaggers a bit about the cell as he flashes the paper. And he did for a minute—but I pocket the license and watching Tom lock the door, brace Lahley. I shove him down the corridor, too, for he's mighty nervous and this lad is bellowing: "Wait till my boss hears of this." And, "You can't lock me up for nothin'." But the second chirp lacks confidence, because he's already in the coop.

It takes half an hour for me to convince Lahley that we've got to make this duck talk. Twice I almost call up the *Daily Star*. Finally he gives in—but he'll have none of it himself—just slip home and plead ignorance if things go wrong. He wrings his hands like an old woman.

"Haddock will have me broke. This lad is One-Eye Dugan—a tough customer—and you won't be able to get him to talk. But Haddock—"

He shakes them withered, matted locks. Lahley sure has his troubles. It's great to be honest, like me, and have an easy conscience. But I pat him on the back and cheer him up.

"If I make him talk he won't dare complain to Haddock—he'll leave town. If he don't talk—well—"

Oh, I didn't want to say too much to Lahley. I was going to give this lad a real old-fashioned Third Degree.

"Just send me a couple of he-men—and go home and sleep," I tell the toy chief.

Lahley keeps shaking his head, like the old father who can't find the money for the mortgage, but he shoots down to me, Captain Harris.

One minute with Harris, and everything is jake. Here is a man who is willing to let his job go to clean the town of filth. How he ever got to be a captain I don't know. Why, he's almost an honest man. Clear eyes, determined chin, broad forehead streaked with gray. Twenty-two years in the harness—pulling against a deadweight. He hated Foster and his gang—but they daren't give him the gate. Harris was the best liked man in town—and the most feared too. I sure smiled a greeting—with Lahley off our hands, we'd get to real business.

For nearly two hours we laid off in the Chief's room, smoking cigars—Mooney too—and a young sergeant whom Harris could trust. I give them my plan quick enough—but the unknown is a great quantity. One-Eyed Dugan could cool his heels below and wonder what had happened to Haddock.

For the fifth time I went over my plan, and for the fifth time Harris shook his head.

"One-Eyed Dugan's a real hard-boiled egg," he said.

"But even a hard-boiled egg has a yellow streak," I told him.

It was that wise crack that made him coddle more to my whole idea. Heart and soul he was with me.

Somewhere, far distant in the town, the hour of midnight struck clearly through the stillness of the night. Never a better time for dirty work, if you're at all melodramatic. We come to our feet—the stage is set—the hour lends atmosphere. One-Eyed Dugan is going to open up like a pig under a gate.

The police sergeant is dressed in a dirty sweater, great muddy, dirty shoes and a long peaked cap that hides his face. I was staging this party—the properties were my idea. The hard-boiled egg in the cell below was going to get his shell cracked—an earful was coming his way. This was the old third degree. In my day I've been—but enough—I'll let you in on the show.

Down the corridor we trot; Tom Mooney has a grip on the made-up sergeant's collar; I trot behind with a long club swinging loosely in my hand; and following, dragging a bit of chain, clanging loudly over the stone floor, is Captain Harris. We don't hurry none as we pass Dugan's barred door. It's his show and he's entitled to see it all.

Dugan starts in to curse and swear—then stops; them mean little eyes of his take in the chain and the club and our determined faces. His brain is working for once. He's thinking—as his great dirty hands clutch at the bars and his mouth hangs open. We don't give him a tumble.

"You won't get a word out of me." The police sergeant sneers, his head well down, his face turned from the searching eyes of Dugan.

I pull a laugh—a laugh that jerks up Dugan's head and slips his fingers the tighter about the bars.

"Lahley's gone home," I chirp. "I never saw the man yet who wouldn't talk for me—get in there!"

There's the clang of the door in a cell the length of the corridor from Dugan's, and the fireworks begin.

Man! it's a great game; would make your blood run cold. The club bangs on the bed—the chain against the wall—and the sergeant does his stuff like a real actor. The screams he lets out would bring your heart into your mouth; and lay it in your hand, for that matter.

Through it all, my voice rings above the din: "Will you talk now?"

And the sergeant's answering, pitiful shriek: "For God's sake don't beat me to death. I don't know—" A few more bangs on the wall with the club. "I don't know nothing."

And me again: "You better think of something—you skunk."

Again the din—the shrieks—my question—a deadly silence—and Captain Harris's hoarse stage whisper.

"Good God, Williams—you've—the man's *dead.*"

"Suppose he is?" My voice rings with anger. "You're not running a day nursery here, are you? No one saw him come—no one need see him go. Somewhere, off on a lonely road—you know the stuff—every day it happens in the city."

Again silence. Now for the final trick—the one that has struck terror to the heart of many a stauncher crook than I take Dugan to be.

A little red paint on the sergeant's smiling face—a scattering of it over my hands—our faces set grim and hard, and we're ready. Tom Mooney and Harris step out, and without a word walk up the corridor to Dugan's cell and take up a position with their backs against Dugan's barred door. It's well done, too—just enough space between their legs for that tough egg to get an eyeful.

And he does—I can hear him gasp as I drag the slumping figure of the sergeant quickly by the door. The scraping of heavy feet over rough stone, the slam of a door at the end of the corridor—the threatening, somber eyes of Harris and Mooney as they turn and look for an instant at the white face behind them, before they slowly follow me down the corridor.

Chapter 9

After that we didn't wait so long. Five minutes at the most—enough for Dugan to fight his battle with himself. His horror of what he had heard and seen—a real, immediate horror against the unknown dangers of betraying Haddock.

My feet come pounding down the corridor—the key turns—the cell door is open—and the great arms of Tom Mooney encircle and hold the frightened, cringing animal of a man that tries to dash out.

"Dugan—" I look down at the pitiable creature who is crouched in one corner of the room, "I want information from you—and I'm going to get it. What do you know about the murder of Howel L. Foster?"

"Nothing." His arms go above his head as I raise the club—"Nothing much."

Sweet words them. If he had simply let it go at "nothing" what could I do? Sock him one maybe, but you can't just beat up a man. Oh, if you're sure—absolutely positive—it's a different matter. But here—was a guess—nothing to go on but this bird's attempt to run me down. Enough maybe. You could hardly put that down to his sporting blood.

I lower my club—fold my arms and stand over him.

"I've got to know all you know. If you lie, I'll get it." I wait a few seconds then. "A good part of the story, I know—I'll check you up. Come—this ain't going to be no petting party."

This guy is sure one weak sister. He's as full of knowledge as an encyclopedia. Good stuff, too, if you're bent on going into the boot-legging business. I give him the hint that I know Haddock was double-crossing Foster—and throw the accusation that Dugan was in on it.

He was, of course—anyone that would try murder, like running me down, must be pretty close to Haddock. You don't pick comparative strangers to kill men for you.

Did I have to egg this smirking, cringing rat on—not me. I had to slow him up—steer him on the right track. He was anxious to tell me everything. And when I told him that if he came clean I'd let him slip out of town on the milk train in the morning, he was about ready to kiss my feet.

In his heart, I think he must have hated Haddock as much as he feared him.

"Haddock pulled the killing," he kept saying over and over, "but I don't know how it was done. He told me the night before that Foster would be dead in the morning. He feared that Foster was going to railroad him back to jail—suspected he was with the hijackers—what Sticker Haddock headed. He just had to kill him."

"Why 'just had to'—then?" I shot the question at him.

"Because of tomorrow night. Haddock simply couldn't risk interference from Foster." One-Eyed Dugan came back quick enough. "A big shipment of stuff is coming through from Canada—over half a million dollars' worth, and—"

"Half a million dollars' worth of booze?" I cut in on him—he seemed frightened enough to be telling the truth—but that's one sweet bunch of liquor.

Dugan looked up—his frightened eyes were crafty—he was getting ready to make a bargain when he saw the club—the bit of chain. Memory of that body being dragged down the corridor came back to him suddenly—the whiteness of his face turned to a pasty yellow. He didn't try to make terms—hide anything—he blurted the truth out quickly.

"Booze was only a side-line." He seemed to sink nearer to the floor. "Snow—happy stuff—opium."

I heard Harris whistle softly behind me. Even the police had not known that. And a half million dollars' worth of drugs could be slipped into a whiskey case.

"Dope, eh?" I never took my eyes off Dugan—never showed surprise. "And the shipment will go through just the same—Foster dead or not?"

"Yep—from Saint Joseph—a little lumber town just over the border—big men up in Canada are in on the deal—Haddock will

128

have charge, now that Foster's—God—what was that—behind you?"

The others turned, I guess—but not me—I was watching Dugan. He couldn't pull an old game like that on me—not in a Police Station anyway.

I heard the door open—footsteps as Harris passed out—then his voice ring out in command.

"Stop—who is it? You—Ed—Harry—" Silence—and the clang of a door.

I half turned—Tom Mooney stood irresolutely in the open doorway.

"Go find Harris—see what the trouble was," I tell him.

Was Dugan after all not playing a part? He was the only one facing the door. Could someone have been in the corridor—someone listening?

"Whom did you see—think you saw?"

I had to shake him several times by the shoulder.

"Just a figure," he gasped. "A low, crouching figure—Haddock maybe."

"Did you see his face, man?"

But he hadn't. It was hard to get him to talk now. But two things I got out of him before Tom Mooney and Captain Harris came back.

One was—that Max Stern, the lad Foster had given me the letter to, would be driving the precious truck tomorrow night. The other was—the place they always halted on the American side, to get their final word that the road was clear to go through. Just where the hijackers would pretend attack and swipe the stuff, Dugan didn't know; but that Haddock would lead them was certain.

Harris and Mooney came back—and Harris was worried. Someone had been in the Police Station—someone had slipped down that corridor—and someone may have listened to what was said. Hot stuff! Some jug—anybody could snoop around in it. The door was locked, to be sure—but Harris found that a window had been broken open in the Chief's room. Now, who would have the crust to do that? Haddock? Maybe. I'd find out later—oh—I had a way, but I kept it under my hat.

Little more information out of One-Eyed Dugan. That Haddock had told him Foster would be dead before morning was the big point. He had met him on the road when he drove to Hillsbury that night.

"They is all good boys in de gang." Dugan shook his head. "A little gun-play they don't mind—but murder—not them—and how could they do it? Haddock knew—Haddock wanted Foster dead—Haddock killed him. He's clever, is Sticker—none better. He done it—and he done it. You better get him now—at once—lock him up tonight or he'll get away from you. He's planning to skip over the border with a dame when this last big trick is pulled. Get him tonight."

Anxious that we get him tonight. Why? Believed him guilty? Maybe—but if Haddock was listening a few minutes before, Dugan's life wouldn't be worth much. Dugan wanted him locked up to protect himself. That was certain. But in the back of my head I believed Haddock did the ice-pick sticking. He should've anyway. And—

"Come—we'll turn you loose. Get up, Dugan," I tell him.

Did his face light up with this offer of freedom? Not much, it didn't. A bit before, he was hollering to get out—now, yep, he was pleading to stay in—just until a little before four-fifteen a.m., when the milk train pulled out of town.

"Let him stay, Williams." Even Harris must have had a suspicion that it was Haddock who listened. "He's been through a lot—why send him to—out tonight?"

"Yes, yes—please." That bird was on his knees again.

But I shook my head. He was only a pawn in the game, and if he got killed—oh—I shrugged my shoulders. He had to go. It was the only way I could find out whether it had been Haddock spying in the Police Station.

One-Eyed Dugan was a rat and had tried to kill me. I couldn't have the same sympathy toward him as the others had. I just dragged him up—shoved him down the corridor and into the night. He wanted his gun—wanted his knife—but he didn't get them. If Haddock had killed Foster, I'd look pretty if Dugan did Haddock in. No money then.

"Hang around the station and keep dark till the train comes in," I tell him. "Perhaps I may protect you."

What a rat he was! He almost kissed my hand at that. Fool too—what interest did I have in him? But I wanted to be around that station and I didn't want him to suspect why—nor expect me to hold his hand and kiss him good-bye when the train went. I had other business at that station.

I gave him a good start—promised to let Harris in on any information I got—and in return received his promise not to arrest that dope outfit unless he got word from me. Then I took a back street and slipped down to the station myself.

One-Eyed Dugan was the only one there, and a pitiful wreck he was. He wanted to duck the light so Haddock wouldn't see him if he trotted down—and yet he was afraid of the dark. He spent his time between the two of them. From some large packing cases I too watched for Haddock. If he had been listening he surely heard that I intended to turn Dugan loose, and that he would slip out of town on the morning train.

I think that Dugan saw me. I didn't try to hide from him. At least, he got more confidence and walked up and down less—stuck more to the shadows, too.

Hours passed—the train drew in—and no Haddock. Dugan swung aboard—a puff—a jerk—the old iron horse rolled out—and no Haddock. Who then had visited that corridor beneath the cop house? I thought that I knew.

Another train—just as I was leaving it—rolled in. It was booked for Montreal—shouldn't stop here—and yet it did. Why? Was someone going to get off—or—?

No station agent—no red light—just that brief stop—a door swung open—a face looked out—and a figure shot across the tracks. One moment in the light only. But I saw him plainly. Lucky I was at that station. Did you guess it? The lad that took that up-train—the lad who was in a devil of a hurry to quit town and make Canada was—yep—Silent Conners. Now, I'll give you all just three guesses who listened outside that jail cell. Conners was booked for Saint Joseph and no mistake. But he hadn't heard all that I heard—no—I knew the dump where those birds rested just after they crossed the border.

It was four-thirty when I crossed the street to my hotel. I was tired, too, and but for a single light which shone dimly through the dirty glass door, the hotel was in darkness.

Luck—superstition—instinct—or was it the faintest shadow outlined across the light. I don't know—take it your own way—but

I threw myself to my knees and turned sharply, gun drawn. No spit of a bullet—but a whizzing sound—a muffled whisper and the pounding of lead against wood above my head. No one had to tell me what had happened—a gun with a silencer had whispered.

I saw him, too—the hunched shoulders—the running figure—it leaped into the touring car that swung around the corner. I might have hit him—probably would—but not a fatal blow. One thing was sure as I pocketed my gun—when I put lead into that lad, it would be two hundred thousand dollars' worth—nothing less. But I nodded in satisfaction. Haddock had tried to kill me. Why? As the kids say, I must have been getting warm. Good enough. No one had heard—I spotted where the bullet had sunk deeply into the thick wood and swung open the door. Nothing to do now but sleep. I had only one rival to fear—Silent Conners—and if he was on his way to Canada, it was a cinch that he couldn't get Haddock while Haddock was still in Middlend. A nod to the sleepy night clerk who dozed in a big office chair, and I turned in. A clear conscience is a great thing—ten minutes later I slept as peacefully as a little child—but one of my fingers was wound about the trigger of a forty-four— which ain't exactly a childish embrace, I'll admit.

Chapter 10

How many times I've resolved to be through with the thinking business and get down to action I don't know. But morning comes— the sun just creeping in the window, if you're at all for poetry—and I lay stretched out on the bed and try to fit in the pieces of the puzzle. One thing is sure—Haddock's working both ends against the middle. He had poor Edgar thinking the Foster dame pulled the ice-picking party, and the dame is evidently coddling to the idea that loving Edgar got a little too playful that night. She'll be worth upward of a million bucks when the estate is settled, and you can't blame both Haddock and the kid for feeling sentimental. If I was a marrying man, I'd—but how the devil did Haddock croak the old boy off? Mind you, I'm not particular as a rule—but Foster was peddling dope—you can't weep when a guy like that goes out—not if you've seen the ravages of dope like I have. Foster's better planted and no mistake.

Haddock did it. But how—HOW—H O W? Then I jump out of

bed and get dressed. It's hardly seven—I'll play detective just once more—interview the little widow before Haddock gets around and puts the damper on that. I rush things—skip breakfast and make the widow's house. It takes some time for the door to open a crack—but I slip my foot in—push back the dame and trot inside.

Mrs. Foster ain't exactly dressed for visitors—and her lips aren't so red nor her cheeks so blooming—and her hair is all done up and frowzy. But it suits me—I ain't looking for a burlesque show, and it's little glimpses of life like this that keep a man single and—and happy.

She squeals a bit—rushes for the phone—acts frightened and worried, but finally don't do anything but flop into a chair and play the baby act. She's just a bit of a doll after all—no guts for killing. For perhaps five minutes I stand silently by and watch her do her stuff.

"What's Haddock to you?" I chirp suddenly.

She starts—sits straight up—then—like a kid who's learned her piece.

"I think we are going to be married."

"Isn't that kind of rushing things—come, why don't you trust me?" I stop—eye her hard—then, "You think Edgar did the killing—don't you?"

She's on her feet now—her eyes dry and blazing—no more of the timid, frightened woman.

"No—I don't—he didn't—and my husband was a—but Edgar never did it. I don't even think it—"

And she stops—she's clever, in a way. She loves Edgar and wants to protect him—but she thinks he did the killing all right.

Oh, it takes time to convince her that I'm her friend. I've never done so much talking and thinking in my life. I tell her that I know Haddock is trying to make her believe that Edgar was the murderer, and that he wasn't.

"But—" she couldn't keep it in, "—why don't Edgar come to see me? I can't go to him—Haddock will—I can't go."

"That's it." I hurry on. "He's made Edgar think you pulled the trick. You're working wrong, woman. I'm trying to help you. Why, if I wanted to, I could hang the crime on Edgar myself. You gave him the key—he was on the ledge that night."

She was thoroughly frightened now. And I played on her nerves. Lied a bit, too.

"I'm your only hope of saving Edgar—the detective, too, will hang the crime on him. But Edgar didn't do it—how could he? How did Haddock explain the deed to you—the door was bolted?"

In sobs now I got the miserable story.

"The door wasn't locked. Haddock only pretended it was—and the crime was committed before—before the policeman was put on guard in the next room. Edgar was on the ledge near the study window when you went to search the house the second time—and while my husband was in bed, Edgar came through the study window—tapped on the bed-room door. Mr.—my husband thought it was the police and opened the door."

More tears and then again— Man! I was all ears.

"Then—then Haddock said Edgar grabbed him—thrust his hand over his mouth—raised the ice-pick and drove it deep into his heart. The body was dragged into the room—the door closed—and Edgar climbed back on the ledge. It all happened in a moment."

Light! I should say so!

"Haddock told you all this—guessed at it?" I held her wrist tightly.

"He saw it." She breathed the words very softly. "He was hunting in the attic—heard a noise and returned just in time to see the murder."

"And why didn't he tell?" I asked.

"Because—oh, he never mentioned it before—he loved me." Down went her head again.

"Little fool," I lifted up her chin, "Edgar never pulled the trick. I saw that ice-pick the first time we searched the house—the second time—well, I don't remember—but Edgar didn't use it."

"Then—how could it happen?"

But I didn't tell her. Haddock's cleverness had gone too far for once; besides, he had confided in a woman. It wasn't the crime of Edgar he had outlined. It was his own. To convince the woman how it could have been done he told the truth. See it—simple—that's why no one noticed it. I had seen the ice-pick the first time we searched the house. Then Haddock came along—copped the pick—suggested we search the house again and slipped above, to the attic. While we were below—and Tom Mooney was with me—bing—like that he had done it just like he described Edgar. Easy—Tom Mooney sat with his gun on his knee all night—and the man was dead. Tom had watched over a corpse. Of course, the coroner was right that the man had been dead at least six hours. Haddock had been the only one to try the door in the morning. In the excitement, Mooney had broken down the door, taking Haddock's word that it was bolted. Such things happen easily, in times of great excitement. To complete the job, Haddock had ripped off the bolt while Tom telephoned the chief.

"I'll be the best man when you marry Edgar," I told her as I dashed out the front door.

What a scene I would make in court—a detective—Race Williams—spilling it all out—deductions—clues—and all that bunk. Back to the hotel for mine. I had beaten out the best detective in the business at his own game. Here I was, in town with Haddock, and the bum dick had gone to Canada. A laugh there. No more thinking now—I ate breakfast in my room, and while the coffee cooled I spent my time cleaning my guns and humming a bit of a tune. Not so bad, you say. Right!

Haddock, in his anxiety to convince the woman that Edgar did the dirt, had overshot the mark. A good meal—a bit of a stretch, and I slipped out into the clear spring morning. Funny how you notice things when your heart is light—and nothing troubling your head. Yep—for the first time I see the green of the grass and the foliage creeping upon the trees. Why not—I was feeling pretty good. Nothing now but to get Haddock—and if he reached for his gun—and then—two hundred thousand dollars ($200,000.00). Looks better—bigger—when all the naughts are down that way. Say it with lead!

Haddock is a sun dodger; so I expect he'll lay in bed until noon. It's ten when I slip up to his house. Nice shed in the back—I walk alongside of that—slip up on the kitchen porch and drop into the kitchen before that single manservant suspects me. Dope! It's written plainly on the sharp features of that little half-wit. Tickling his ribs with my gat don't get a word out of the servant—threats fall dead. Then I get it—the bird's a dummy. He smiles knowingly when I find that out, but I wipe the grin off his distorted map when I hand him a pencil. I ain't out to ask questions. Nothing but action goes now.

A hand on his throat—the business end of the gat between his teeth and he does his lessons like an A.1. pupil. Haddock has gone to Canada. A search of the house does no good. Get it? The dick has beaten me. Yep—just when everything was set. The curtain was up for the final act and—hell—Haddock and Conners were both in Canada.

Mad? I don't know. Pride goeth before a fall—but I had taken one awful tumble. I could see it all clearly now, as I leave the house. Too much thinking. All along I knew Haddock did the killing. See the point—I should have bumped him off and hunted up how he did the crime afterward. But suppose the dopey dummy was lying? I'd search the town—trot around all Haddock's hangouts. Wouldn't I look pretty when Silent Conners sent in his telegram:

"Coming home with the remains."

My search of the town was a fliv—Haddock had skipped clean. And I buy the paper. Man! when I see the glaring headlines spread all across the front of that sheet I was mad enough to bite myself.

$5,000.00 REWARD—DEAD OR ALIVE
For the Murderer of Our Esteemed Citizen, Howel L. Foster.
The police of our fair city intend to spare no—

B-r-r-r. And it was I who was protecting Conners from any retribution for his shooting.

Beaten—eh—that was what made me sit up. There was a chance yet—perhaps—but, Man! we would be playing it close. I'd—

Came one of those ideas that hit a man out of a clear sky. I turned into the jewelry shop down the street from Farrington's. What did I get there—oh—for one thing I bought a cheap watch to take the place of the one left in Farrington's. That it took me over two hours to get it is my business.

There ain't much of a hurry now—my game is a waiting one until dusk anyway. I keep clear of Harris and Tom Mooney, though they make several attempts to get in touch with me. But I do write them a letter—a letter to be delivered to Harris at twelve o'clock that night.

That it looks bad for me, I'll admit—but I'm going to make one more bid for that bank roll. I think I see a way to meet Haddock just as soon as Conners—sooner—yes. Haddock would never allow himself to be taken alive, and the man who shoots first, wins—and the prize is a good one.

Chapter 11

As a rule I go easy with my money, but now I trot and buy a secondhand Ford for about sixty bucks more than it's worth. It's a good car, and I'm not buying someone else's trouble—I have troubles enough of my own. Just at dark the tub and I slip out of town. I've got Foster's letter to Max Stern and a good mental picture of just where that shack in the woods is that the liquor car gets its final word that all is safe.

I wasn't always a city chap—not me. I know my country, and I've got a good sense of direction. It'll be less than sixty miles—with fifty-five of it soft going—villages and farmhouses for identification. Me and the Ford make time.

Every house is a blue book and I have no trouble. There, far off in the lonely, wooded countryside, I park my Ford under some trees and hunt for that shack. That's the hard part—not a hundred yards from the road, I've been told by Dugan, and yet it took me the best part of two hours to find it. It's low—half sunk into a hillside, with two windows—one on either side—and a heavy barred door. No light from within—that's the reason I missed it and never would have stumbled on it if it wasn't for the sudden glare of a lantern—the rough, unshaven countenance of a great giant of a man who stepped out the door and looked into the clearness of the night.

He just stood there shaking his head. Didn't like the weather, I guess. And I too was worried—suppose the truck didn't come through? Get my idea? Haddock was going to hold up that truck—and I—why, I intended to be aboard it. If I couldn't find Haddock I'd let him find me. That Mountain and Mohammed business that used to be in the school reader.

Twice I trained my gun on him—ready to step out—and twice I hesitated. Max Stern would be on the truck, and this baby would be hard to convince of anything. But I had to do it—I stepped closer, drew a bead right between his eyes, and spoke from the shadows.

"Just a moment, friend." If his face turned white, you couldn't tell, it was so dirty and matted with thick brush. And then— "If you pull that gun you're reaching for, you'll take it to hell with you."

That fetched him—them sweet words he understood. His hand came from his hip and came empty. The best part of the next five minutes was spent in convincing him that I was a friend. This friendly stuff was getting to be a regular habit with me lately.

Into the house we walked all right—him pulling at his whiskers and trying to work that dead gray matter under his matted hair. Once inside, I gave him the office—handed him Foster's letter introducing me to Max Stern.

He hadn't been to college, but he studied out the words, spelling some of them aloud and scowling at me when I helped him out. Then I talked.

At first I couldn't get anything out of him except: "Foster's dead—he'll be dead several days now."

This bird was sure thick. Did he think I was trying to push off a spirit message on him? Luckily we had lots of time and he was willing to believe most anything bad of Haddock. Take it all around, Haddock was not very well liked. When I explained the double-crossing by Haddock and how the truck was going to be held up this night, he flew into a rage and I had to stick my gun in his chest and start all over again. But he was willing that I take it up with Max, who'd drive the truck. Max was coming through alone—this big lad would climb aboard there—two on a truck was the limit—more looked suspicious. But if hijackers were on the road we'd take, and Haddock was among them—well—he shook his dirty locks and muttered: "We'll see what Max has to say."

And that was that—a fine pair we made sitting there waiting for the rumble of the truck across the old bridge up the road.

Two hours later it came—distant but distinct—like a flash we were out—dashing toward the road—the lantern waving. And the truck drew up.

The driver stepped down—cursed softly as he saw me—and then another man climbed from the truck to stretch his legs. Gad—I seldom show surprise, but this time I couldn't help it. Silent Conners had come through with the truck from Canada. Get it—that lad was there. But I breathed easier too—we started even, now, on our hunt for Haddock.

Max Stern read my letter in the dim light, while Conners and I eyed each other. It was funny in a way—and Conners was smiling—as he easily fingered his watch chain. I grinned too. Fair's fair—I'll take an even break with any man.

Max Stern could reason—think things out for himself.

"I've heard of you, Race Williams," he says, putting out a mit. "I don't know your game nor why you're here, but if it's true about Haddock and the hijackers, we'll need several quick guns tonight. That you're not working in with the police is a cinch." He smiled meaningly. "But—Haddock—yes, I have suspected him. Perhaps you've got the same reason for coming aboard as this lad has," and he jerked a thumb toward Conners. "Personal grudge against Haddock—wants a bit of shooting."

I nodded grimly—part of that was true—about the bit of shooting—but how had Conners got aboard? Did Max Stern know he was a dick from the city? And—but I couldn't tell that to Max—I couldn't get him suspecting both of us. For the same reason, I suppose Conners didn't try lying about me and trying to keep me from being one of the party. No—too much talk would kill things. As it was—well, we all four climbed aboard the truck.

It was Conners who suggested that he and I slip into the back of the truck and keep low.

"If they see four men, they may not make the attack," he told Max.

"Then we get through clean," Max grinned. "But I suppose you want your chance at Haddock—all right—if he gets put out I get his job. Shoot to kill."

"I will." Conners nodded vigorously. "Me and my little shadow will slip behind these *oil* barrels." And we did—as for me, the time for talking was over—the reward read "dead or alive"—my lead had to get home first.

Zip—we were off, speeding through the night.

Ten minutes at the most we shot down the grade, onto the level for a short stretch and up a little hill. Then all hell broke loose. These hijackers shouted no command—just cold-blooded murder was what it was. A dozen shots blazed out at once—peppered against the cases—shattered the glass in the front.

Came the grinding of brakes—a shot or two from the front seat—a muffled curse—the thud of a falling body—and the car stopped. Four masked men were crowding around the car. Conners and I stood up together.

I think a bullet seared my face but I ain't sure—but, man! we let them have lead—three tumbled in less than thirty seconds—the fourth turned and sped into the forest. The fight was over—but—I didn't bother with the masked men on the ground. I've got an eye

SAY IT WITH LEAD!

for figures, I have—and Haddock had gone into the woods. It was Conners who paused to tear off the masks—I was beating through the bush, on the heels of Haddock. If anyone cursed the moonlight now, I was not that one. Twice I saw him—and as I raised my gun he disappeared again behind the trees. Then I lost him—struck a clearing a few minutes later—saw his figure dash into the woods on the other side. He was gaining on me but that didn't matter. I even slowed up on my pace—he was traveling toward the little shack. He'd make his last stand there. I chuckled softly—no sound behind me—Conners was completely off the track.

Chapter 12

I found the house—approached it carefully—snaking through the luxurious growth of mountain grass. Not a light—not a sign of life—just a somber, eerie stillness. The windows—yes—but the moon was up and I'd be plainly visible. I slipped up the side of the mountain—slid down upon the little flat roof—saw a figure—pulled my gun and faced another. Came a soft, mocking laugh.

"You're always late but you get there just the same, eh?" Conners whispered softly. Then—"Be careful of that gun of yours, Race Williams—there isn't any money wrapped up in my hide."

Always beating me to it. How did he know that Haddock would seek the house? Why, there wasn't any certainty that he was in there now.

"He's going to fight to a finish. The man who shoots first wins," I told Conners grimly. "Now, how to get in—how to know that he's here."

"Easy."

Conners laughed. Turning, he crawled slowly to the edge of the little roof by the front of the house. For the first time, I noticed the axe by his side. Leaning over, he struck the top of the wooden door below a vicious blow—then another and another. The door creaked—a bit of wood flew out in the moonlight and we knew that Haddock was inside. A pistol had spoken—a bullet crashed through the door. Haddock was using heavy lead now.

But the time for caution had passed. Too much money was involved. I'd let Conners play his foxy trick of hanging on the roof—as for me, I'd try a window. Without a word I dropped from the roof—slid along the little shed, from which Conners must have lifted that axe, and dropped to the ground. If Conners didn't get his man in three minutes, he'd be too late. The curtain would be rung down on the final act. If Haddock wanted to take a pot shot at me, he was welcome to it. Which all goes to show that two hundred thousand dollars don't grow on trees. Besides, I was a bit sick of having Conners bob up ahead of me.

No wasted time now—I just twist my gun—slip down beneath the window and, raising my arm, club the glass out of it. Do I expect a bullet through my wrist? I don't know—if I do get one I'll shower that room with so much lead that Haddock will look like he had porous-knit underwear on when we pick him up.

The glass goes to the floor—not much noise—must have fallen on a bed—yep—I remember now, there was one under the window. No shot—no sound—what's happened to Haddock? I come up straight and slant through the window. It's dark—deadly dark—in there. Well, I'll chance it—I lift my electric torch and shoot a ray into the room. I'm desperate. I saw Conners do a bit of pretty shooting back there on the truck.

Gun ready—the light splashed into the room. It's as empty as a senator's hat. No place to hide—not a sign of life. Another one of them hidden mysteries. Gad—let's go—I stick up a foot; give a bit of a hoist; and I'm in—in and alive. Then I know—as I press out my light a splash of moonlight slips into the room—from the roof, near the back. There's a trap door, leading above, and it's open. A minute—less than that—and I'm on that ladder, climbing to the roof. All the time Conners is a-pounding on that front door—bent on crashing it down and plugging Haddock as he runs out. Comes a dull thud—a groan—and I stick my head into the moonlight. Conners is stretched silent on the tarred boards. Above him loom the broad shoulders of Haddock. His gun is raised to strike again—beat out the helpless man's brains. And the ladder squeaks—Haddock turns. I find out then how quick he is, as a pain shoots up my right arm and my gun tumbles through the trap into the room. And Haddock finds how quick I am—quick and sure—my left gun barks once—just that sudden flash of orange-blue flame, and Haddock does his stuff—tumbles from the roof.

I wasn't in good position to shoot maybe—and the sudden pain in my right arm jarred me up considerably—but I'll lay even money that they'll find that bullet within—oh, say, an eighth of an inch of Haddock's heart.

And Conners isn't hurt bad—he's up and staggering about the roof, trying to get at the truth of the matter. But he comes through like a man, and thanks me for saving his life. That's gratitude and I appreciate it, but I relieved him of both his guns—Haddock might not feel dead and I'm not the one to put temptation in the way of any man. The trust fund is to be paid to the man who captures Haddock dead or alive. I'm just cautious—never leave any loopholes. When I do a job—but we drop through the trap, slip out the front door, and drag Haddock in.

Conners is too much interested in the lad's condition—he works over him while I light the lanterns. I'm not a doctor—there's no hurry either—one look at Haddock and I know it's only a matter of time before he's handed in his final papers. But he comes to and curses me. Nothing else matters—he just hates me. Don't mind dying—the only thing that bothers him is that I live and collect.

Conners seems a good sport—damned if he don't get Haddock to write a confession of the crime. That's good—I'd have hard work explaining it. So I let them alone and hang up a couple of lanterns outside—one by the door—one down near the road. It's near one o'clock and my letter to Captain Harris told him to hunt me up at the little shack as soon as he received that letter. You see—I didn't know what might happen there—and it was the best meeting place—I wanted him to make the pinch of the truck.

I get back as Haddock finishes his confession. Once again he raises his voice—sneers—curses and yells: "You'll never—never get—get—"

And that's that. Haddock's burst of passion hurries the inevitable and he checks out—he's as dead as the prohibition amendment. The dick from the city is a good fellow—I'll slip him ten grand, and I tell him so.

Conners seems all in—nodding there in the corner by the side of the dead man—watching me from beneath drooping head. But I don't bother about the confession—better for him to turn it over to the police—won't look like I forced it out of Haddock. There may be some trouble collecting. But—I'll get what's coming to me. I always do.

An hour later Harris and Mooney and Lahley find the little

shed—and the wise mouth-piece, Marston, is with them.

"There's your man," I say. "Now—get me to town—I need something for my wrist."

The crowd looks Haddock over, and helps Conners to his feet.

"Conners has his confession," I say lightly.

And I watch Conners hand it over to Chief Lahley while Marston's eyes nearly bulge out of his head. It's a great night for me and no mistake. What's a shattered wrist to a man of my—coming wealth?

"You can make the pinch."

I tell Harris where the truck is and the dope too. But they're all interested in that paper.

It's Lahley and Harris that walk over and lay a couple of kindly hands upon my shoulders.

"Too bad, Williams," Harris says, "you didn't get here in time to shoot first."

But I laughed.

"Never mind that—I got him—Conners is my witness."

"Conners says he did it."

Lahley leans over anxiously.

"He lies—" Like a flash my gun was out, and if Lahley hadn't been in the way Conners wouldn't have made no more foolish statements. "Anyway, he can't prove it."

"But he can." Marston chirps with glee. "Look—"

And as the others held my arms Marston shows me Haddock's confession. There it was all right—just how he committed the crime—but at the bottom—at the bottom. Why, Conners, the damned skunk, had got Haddock to write out a statement that he (Conners) had shot him. Conners, whose life I had saved—and Haddock—oh, I guess he hated me enough to do it.

"Too bad," I heard Harris say through a thick haze of passion. "For once you're beaten, Race."

Damned, but it sure did look that way. Without a word I let Tom Mooney take me and lead me to the Ford. Back to town we drove together—Lahley and Harris and the cops going after the truck. What became of Conners and Marston I didn't know—and didn't care much either. And in his confession, Haddock had described the killing just as he had told it to Mrs. Foster—only he used the ice-pick instead of Edgar. Tough—I had doped that out.

Chapter 13

You think that's the end—that Race Williams is flat on his back—counted out while a couple of cheap crooks—a lawyer and a city dick—split the pile. Take another guess. I'm sticking close to Middlend. Yep—I'm a witness to the killing—Marston has added insult to injury and offered me—but listen.

He sails in one day, his cane swinging, a white carnation in his button hole. He put that there himself, but he don't know that I'm thinking of laying a lily in his hand. And that ain't maybe.

"You're done, Williams." He puts on his briskest air. "But we're big-hearted—my client and I—next Wednesday is the day set for the payment. I've arranged things with the Trust Company—there'll be a representative with the check. No fuss, you understand." He looked hard at me as he pointed his stick at my chest. "Big-hearted, did I say? Yes—that's it. If—aw—if you make no trouble—tell the truth—the right truth—there'll be something in it for you. Nothing in writing, you understand—but Conners says you helped him a bit—a gratuity—say—aw—five—well, perhaps ten thousand."

I stood and looked at him but said nothing. The dirty little swindler. He thought—well—he feared I'd croak one of them off, I guess—and I don't know—under certain circumstances he might have been right.

"You'll be there—Wednesday—twelve noon. Otherwise you can't get anything, no matter what you claim—rather thoughtful of Haddock—poor chap—rather thoughtful." He edged nearer the door.

But I didn't kick him out. I nodded—then: "I'll be there."

I was going to get all I could. Think that one out yourself, gentle or hard-boiled reader.

The papers were full of the shooting—Conners had been exonerated from all liability and made a hero. All Haddock's dirt was published—Captain Harris got a big hand for capturing the dope laden truck. Foster, being in too close with the officials, was just a victim of his public spirited zeal to stamp out the bootleggers and drug peddlers. And at the end of the glowing accounts—way at the bottom—third page—stuck to one side of the third picture of Conners was the final fling.

Tom Mooney, former local officer, and one Race Wilson, from out of town, participated in the final events of that hectic evening.

Gad! They didn't even get my name right. A few years—when I was a bit younger I'd've shot up a newspaper office for that—but now I just shrugged my shoulders—kept close to my hotel room and saw no one but Tom Mooney. Good old faithful Tom Mooney—and Harris, too, if I'd let him come to the hotel. But I wouldn't. As for Lahley—he was up to his old tricks—kissing the ground behind the winner.

Came the fatal Wednesday noon, as they say in the movies. And with it I trotted down to the bank building—the paying of the huge check was to be private—but the street was blocked with people—like all confidential stuff in small cities.

Lahley was there—Marston—three men from the bank—and in the back Mrs. Foster and Farrington—also up against a side wall, in the shadows, the worn old face I was looking for—never mind who—you'll get it later.

Mooney and Harris came in together—a few minutes' wait—wild cheers from without. Three policemen battered against the crowd and finally closed the door. Marston and Conners strolled down the room. Playing for the gallery—well, I didn't blame them for that. Scornfully Conners looked at me—but I gave him eye for eye. My look registered too, for a minute later the cops came over and took my gats. I made no fuss. I was ready.

The bank man was one of those gray-haired, somber, honest ducks. He adjusted his glasses, introduced the lawyer from the city, who had charge of the trust fund—spoke about expenses—argued a bit with Marston—settled on the amount, I guess—then made a speech, laying down the terms of the trust in a few thousand words, where ten would have done it. Then he looked up—beamed on us—and wanted to know if anyone questioned the legal right of Conners to receive the money.

And I did. Just came to my feet and jerked it out.

"Why, Conners was lying on his back with a gash across his head where the bandage is now." I pointed at Conners. "Haddock was going to do him in when I shot. I saved his life—killed Haddock—and took this." I held up my damaged wrist.

Conners was half on his feet, glaring at me—it was the first time I ever really saw him mad. Marston was hissing in my ear that I wouldn't get "a damned cent"—and Harris and Mooney had drawn close to the long table.

145

"Everything set, Harris?" I whispered.

He nodded quickly, squeezing my arm. Then to the banker and the lad who clutched at a check, a pen wavering in his hand, "May I ask a few questions?"

"Certainly."

These bankers are all very affable gents. Why shouldn't they be, always taking their gambles with someone else's money.

"Good! You have the bullet there that was taken from the body of Haddock."

"Yes."

"Just one bullet."

"Yes, the bit of lead is here. The doctor turned it over to me."

"What caliber is it?"

"Forty-four. The same as Mr. Conners uses."

"Well—it's my bullet, not his," I say simply.

"But, my dear sir." He gave the impression of being very patient—though the trust lawyer smiled up at me. "Haddock has signed an ante mortem statement—written it in his own hand—that Conners killed him."

Then I threw the bomb—just hurled it at that crowd—get this: "Here." I tossed him a strong magnifying glass that Harris slipped into my hand. "Read aloud what you find on that chunk of lead. Read it—you dumb head."

I just couldn't help bawling him out when he stood there looking vacantly at me. But that got him—he picked up the glass—looked through it absently a moment—then his eyes bulged.

"Good and loud," I told him, but I wasted my breath.

He just bellowed it. He shrieked aloud the tiny letters cut upon the lead.

"R—" he paused. "W—what does that mean?" he gasped.

"It means that I'm no fool." I banged my fist down on that table. "It means that when I leave here I'm going to—" I glanced at Conners and Marston, "but literally it means—pay to the order of Race Williams—Two Hundred Thousand Dollars. Those are my initials on the slug. Now—do you know whom that bullet belongs to?"

And they did.

Conners and Marston started a holler but they stopped dead. There was no chance to accuse me of framing the lead. The jeweler who cut it in the bullet for me was the worn old face in the corner of the room. Harris and three others had seen it extracted from the dead Haddock. My case was complete. Luck! Man—when I play for big stakes I don't need luck. Why hadn't I acted before—oh—well—why have trouble in the town—Marston had gone into the legal end of it and proved that the actual killer was within his rights as a deputy sheriff.

Conners and Marston tried to put up a front—but Harris stopped them.

"Listen."

He raised a hand and held it so until everybody in the room was deadly quiet.

From the street came the cry of newsboys—young salesmen peddling their wares in that crowd without.

"Extrey—*Daily Star*—all about the shooting of Haddock—Race Williams gets full credit—bullet identified—Marston and Conners, crooks—Extrey."

And that was all. There was a back door and Conners and Marston were glad to make use of it. But they confessed first—just the threat of turning them over to the howling mob. An angry, surging mob threatening to lynch the very man they had been worshiping for the past few days. That's mob psychology and not bad stuff either.

How did I do it? A cinch. Two hundred grand is a lot of money. I don't take chances with so much coin. The little lad who had charge of the trust was in on the know from the first finding of the bullet. He didn't like Marston and let me work it out my own way. As for the *Daily Star*—well, we let them have a slant at the bullet—the tiny initials on condition they wouldn't have their paper on the street before twelve-thirty.

Before we were finished there Lahley got his promised cut in—and I slipped Tom and Harris a pretty sum—nothing stingy. When I cleared the bank building, well, I was over a hundred grand to the good. Not so bad for a couple of weeks work.

The end—yep—just about. There was a special train waiting for me at the station. Oh, I don't specially like to be glorified, but a little advertisement don't hurt my business. Out of town papers please copy.

Ben Boulden is a long-time book reviewer and commenter on the crime fiction world, lately turned novelist with two entries in the Blaze! *series of adult westerns,* Red Rock Rampage *(2017) and* Spanish Gold *(2017), both published by Rough Edges Press. For the past year he's written the "Short & Sweet: Short Stories Considered" column for* Mystery Scene Magazine. *Ben's lived in Connecticut and now Utah with a wife, a daughter, a dog, and a fish.*

A Calculated Risk
Ben Boulden

Six years, two months, thirteen days.

Nothing more than a measurement of time's passage. The spread so large it would be impossible to connect the perpetrator with the crime. Only a fool or madman would hold a grudge so long. A grudge most never knew existed and those who did know, would have forgotten years ago. It wasn't much of a thing anyway.

An everyday betrayal.

One man with power, the other without. Words whispered in boardrooms, meeting halls, offices, cubicles, telephone conversations. Rumors from a single source—

...trouble at home... finances... gambling... angry... sick... he dropped the ball... can't do the job anymore... I heard...

"I heard." The whispered rumors scuttled from person to person until everyone had heard something. The powerless man heard the whispers too; he began doubting himself. His skill, his competence, even his intelligence. His hands started shaking conspicuously. His palms became sweaty. He stuttered when he talked. He—

...lost his wife, his daughter. His home.

Everything.

He moved to a rundown apartment on the west side. A three-hundred-square-foot studio. The walls paper thin. His neighbors drug addicts, hookers and dealers. He listened to their music, idiotic laughter, moronic conversations, grinding and obscene lovemaking.

But it was the whispers that awakened him in the night. The sound of his betrayal. His lost reputation. His...

Then four years ago everything changed. An idea struck in the godless hours of a Monday as he awaited an alarm clock's chime to signify another meaningless day spent at a pointless job.

He began to plan.

His revenge would be cold, calculated.

He shaved, cut his hair, purchased new clothing with his pre-paid credit card—a suit, three oxford shirts, Florsheims, a fashionable tie. He updated his resumé, found a new job. A general ledger accounting position in the corporate office of a regional grocery chain. He did well and was promoted to director of accounts payable, then to assistant controller and finally controller. His salary moved steadily higher. He found a more comfortable apartment in a cozy east side neighborhood.

He contacted his ex-wife—who still lived in his house, in an exclusive neighborhood on Salt Lake City's east bench—and tried to arrange a meeting with his daughter.

"Fuck you, Harry."

Then silence as the digital line went vacant.

It didn't matter. Nothing mattered except the plan.

From a metered parking space across the street, Harry watched the powerful man leave his office in the evenings. The meter always paid with cash, the car in a different spot each time. Harry noted with some glee that the powerful man had gained weight over the preceding years. An extra chin beneath a salt and pepper beard. His button-down office shirt always pinched at the belt, the placket twisted in revolt against his expanding belly, underarms stained with sweat. And, Harry thought, the same bovine look as always in his eyes.

The man's departures were haphazard. Some evenings he would stroll from the building at five o'clock and others it would be eight or nine. Except Fridays. On Friday the man was as faithful to three o'clock as a whore to her pimp. The only other constant was the way in which the fat man departed. He crashed through the doors, looked briskly to his left and right, walked directly to his car two blocks away where he opened its door and tumbled behind the wheel in an almost uncontrolled fall and drove away.

Harry planned the murder as he would prepare a cost proposal for his employer. One step at time, every detail identified and accounted for. Contingencies planned with second-, third- and fourth-tier alternatives—in this case, escape routes, shooting locations, alibis and explanations.

Harry's risk of discovery by the police low, and the reward of success, the revenge Harry wanted, almost guaranteed.

The plan simple.

A mugging in the dark alley used by the fat man as a shortcut between two brick buildings near block's end. One building vacant. The other, a restaurant, open only for lunch. No lights, no cameras, and no witnesses on a cold winter night. There would be two shots. The first, a panicked blast to the fat man's belly and the second, more deliberate, as if the mugger decided the dead are worse witnesses than the living, in his chest. The victim's wallet, watch and briefcase gone.

Another senseless murder in a city brimming with drugs and violence.

Two years before the planned murder, Harry purchased a .38 revolver through a newspaper ad. He practiced faithfully, in an isolated desert canyon, always alone, until becoming proficient enough to hit anything of size within fifteen yards. Then Harry put the gun away and waited, watching the fat man go about his daily business.

Next came the cosmetics and facial prosthetics. Harry purchased, with cash, a Hollywood Makeup Kit from a Santa Barbara beauty shop while on vacation.

A toothy, father-like smile on his face, Harry told the cashier, "My daughter will love this."

A cheap pair of running shoes, two sizes too small, changed Harry's gait. The resulting jerky walk fit the fat man's mugger perfectly. A luckless drug addict unable to even perform a simple mugging without fucking up. Harry's alter-ego was named Todd. Stupid, callous, and eager for his next fix. Nothing else mattered. Not even the life of a chubby junior executive walking to his car after work.

Harry became unrecognizable.

Then one crisp October evening as Harry watched, the fat man did something unexpected. Instead of turning left and walking to his car, he turned right. His stride faster than normal. His gaze affixed to the cold concrete sidewalk.

From across the street, Harry followed.

The fat man walked down Broadway. He didn't raise his head until he reached 300 West where he stopped, looked over his shoulder furtively, eyes wide. A cell phone appeared in his hand. Its harsh blue light visible from where Harry stood in a copse of trees next to a Residence Inn.

With his thumb and forefinger, the fat man tapped the phone's screen. He stared at the device intently. His tongue escaped the corner of his mouth. After a moment, a creeping smile ruptured his puffy face. He looked across the intersection at Pioneer Park—a one-block tree-filled oasis for the homeless, where prostitutes and drug dealers worked deals without harassment from the police—to where a young woman stood, dressed in a skin-tight, thigh-high red dress, black net stockings, blonde hair piled into a modified beehive, waving at the fat man.

Harry smiled.

His plan changed.

A quick cold death would be too easy for the fat man. The man with enough power and rat-like cunning to topple Harry's life. A man who made his bones in the company at Harry's expense. A man Harry despised more than he could have imagined only a few years before.

Harry watched the man lumber across the street and exchange greetings with the prostitute. He leaned into the woman—searching for a kiss, Harry thought—only to be rebuffed. The hooker held her hand out; Harry heard her words clearly across the chilled night.

"One-fifty." She posed, hands on hips, her head moving back and forth with each word. "Now."

The fat man raised his hands. He said something Harry couldn't hear; ended with his nauseating over-loud laugh and reached for his wallet. A few bills passed between palms and the woman took the fat man's hand and led him deeper into the park.

Harry followed as they moved under a cottonwood at the park's back edge, next to a childless playground and worn-out tennis court.

The woman sank to her knees, unbuckled the fat man's belt. His pants dropped to the cold ground. His legs pale, grotesque. With her right hand, the prostitute stroked something too small for Harry to see. She looked up and whispered a few words that made the fat man smile, giggle. She moved her mouth to his groin, and began a smooth, expert motion.

And Harry caught it all on video. Every moan. Every groan. Every last second of the shameless act.

The next day, Harry drove two hours to a Walmart north of Salt Lake City where he purchased a mass-produced thumb drive. He wore a simple disguise, paid cash. He transferred the video from his cell phone to his computer, washing away any identifying markers, and downloaded it to the thumb drive.

He mailed the drive, and its contents, to the fat man's wife in a plain manila envelope. No note or anything else that could be used to identify him as the sender.

And he waited.

A month later, Harry heard from a former co-worker—a chatty woman who had kept in touch—about the fat man's pending divorce.

He feigned disinterest.

Harry felt content, almost happy. This euphoric wellness lasted two months before the whisperings began awakening him again.

Anger. Anxiety.

But for Harry it was mostly shame that kept sleep away. The shame of allowing a half-wit dung beetle like Jerry to destroy everything he had built. The fat man, Jerry, had taken his job, his daughter, his wife.

Now it was Harry's turn. Again. He was still owed a debt from Jerry's betrayal and the account needed balancing.

Harry took the flimsy calendar from the wall of his small home office. A room at the back of his new house. This house larger than the last and located in a more exclusive section of town. A house that made his ex-wife spitting mad and caused her as many tears as she caused him legal problems.

Harry walked through the calendar before stopping at November. The exact day to be determined. A nice cold month. Dark, too. A time of year his alter-ego Todd would be desperate for a warm place to stay. A fix. And money to buy both.

In June, Harry began shadowing Jerry again—who had slimmed to saggy-flesh skinny after his nasty divorce. His hours more consistent now as he commuted to a small apartment on the west side. Once a month the sallow man made a detour to Pioneer Park for a dance with a blonde beehive. But Harry didn't film the trysts. Instead he sat in his BMW parked across the street and watched the herky-jerky motion of the prostitute's head. A warm feeling of accomplishment in his belly though it wasn't enough.

And when Harry's desk calendar flipped to November 8, he knew the game would soon be over.

His day had arrived.

Harry left his office at the usual time. Not early or late because people never remembered the usual, but always recalled the unusual.

He drove home, parked the BMW in the garage, and transformed into Todd before driving to meet Jerry in a dark alley connecting Broadway and 400 South.

The high-pitched squeal like a well-played piece of music, as the first bullet found Jerry's stomach. A putrid odor made it clear an intestine had been ruptured.

Todd smiled, Harry said, "You motherfucking piece of shit," spittle splattering on the alley's cold, black asphalt. "You see me, Jerry? I win, you lose."

Jerry's final word a blessing, since it made clear his understanding of Harry's victory: "You?"

Harry basked in the moment, counted to three before Todd leveled the .38 at Jerry's left eye, and pulled the trigger again.

The long silence after, as brilliant as what had come before.

Todd removed the skinny man's wallet, his watch—a shitty plastic Casio—and snatched the cheap faux leather briefcase from the crusty asphalt. He walked at what a junkie would think was a normal pace. After turning the corner, Todd moved west on Broadway for two blocks, stopped in the vestibule of an abandoned deli and disappeared.

Three minutes later, Harry appeared at the deli's side exit. He walked to the BMW with a brisk, determined step, opened its trunk, placed the wallet, watch and briefcase in a black plastic garbage bag. Tossed Todd's clothes and the .38 on top and closed the trunk's lid with a satisfying thud.

He opened the driver-side door and slid behind the wheel.

With a push of a button, the engine's velvet purr caught fire.

Harry buckled his seatbelt. He closed his eyes.

When he looked back at the world, everything seemed fresh, hopeful. The city more vivid, its lights brighter, than it had been in years. The world was shining in the dark.

Harry wanted to celebrate his victory, but the emotion was dangerous. Any deviation from the plan would create problems.

Before pulling away from the curb, Harry waited for a break in the midweek evening traffic. Another anonymous car in a crowded commute, working its way home to dinner and a few hours of television.

Harry followed the escape route he had mapped so many years ago, merged onto I-15 and then I-80. Drove west twenty-five miles to Lake Point Junction where he exited the interstate and followed a frontage road.

Not another car in sight.

To his left, Saltair, a decaying nineteenth-century Mormon-built resort with a Moorish design, crouched against the dark sky and farther back was the southern shore of the Great Salt Lake.

Harry drove a mile to an abandoned old-fashioned passenger train car. Its enclosed interior used by middle-class teenagers as a place to drink, dope and have sex. A weekend destination that, as Harry knew it would be, was abandoned on a cold November night.

Behind the passenger car, an eclectic mixture of clothing was scattered across the ground. Harry discarded Todd's shirt, pants and shoes. As planned, they were separated carefully; one shoe tossed into thick sagebrush, the other under the train car. With careful nonchalance the pants and shirt went in two separate piles.

The briefcase and wallet were soaked with lighter fluid, dropped into an empty fifty-five-gallon drum hidden from the road. A match flamed and the cheap materials blistered, burned to ash. Harry smashed the cheap nondescript watch with the heel of his shoe, leaving it in the alkaline dirt to rot.

In the BMW, Harry drove two miles west. The road changed from asphalt to dirt. He stopped three yards from a towering black rock formation, walked to the shoreline, the ground hard under his feet, and tossed the .38 into the sluggish water.

For a moment, Harry watched the lake's slow rolling waves, inhaled its briny odor, and listened to the interstate's hum.

He sauntered back to the car, opened its door, slid behind the wheel. The satisfaction of his accomplishment warm in his belly.

The emotion intoxicating.

Harry pumped his fists, shouted: "Fuck you, Jerry! Fuck you, you motherfucking asshole!"

The BMW whispered to life. Harry backed away from the black rock, turned the car's nose back to where he had come from. He pushed the accelerator, his hands steel clamps on the steering wheel. The satisfying clang of showering rocks against the undercarriage.

A smile on his face for the life he had recovered.

A powerful lust in his belly.

There would be a new wife. This one younger, prettier than the last. Blonde. A new family, two children. A boy and a girl.

Harry passed Saltair, merged onto I-80. He glided left, the accelerator on the floor.

His mind racing, the car's speedometer marking his passage: *100...*

Harry would fuck the auburn-haired receptionist at the office.

...110...

Find a better job, maybe open his own CPA firm.

...120...

Buy an even bigger house, in an even better neighborhood.

...125...

The car's smooth acceleration deceptive, the road's lines softened with speed.

The interstate curved right, the horizon skewed with light as Salt Lake City appeared in the distance.

The BMW skidded, its rear wheels lost traction. The back end sailed left, slammed against the concrete barrier.

The car shuddered, metal screeching against concrete, sparks flying.

The steering wheel useless in Harry's hands, as the car's momentum carried it to the barrier's top edge, where it flipped, landed hard on its roof, sliding thirty feet across the highway's median before stopping.

A dust trail rising in its wake.

The humming traffic obscured Harry's silence. His eyes open, head turned at a killing angle.

In the distance, a siren shimmered to life.

Next Issue

Two issues down, hopefully a bunch more to go. Next time we are very pleased to announce a feature story by international thriller star Barry Lancet with his character, Jim Brodie. Imagine if Robert Ludlum's Jason Bourne had washed ashore on the coast of Japan and become a PI instead of heading off to Switzerland and physics conferences—you might have a hint as to what's in store. Don't miss it.

Cheers,

BOOKS

On the following pages are a few
more great titles from the
Down & Out Books publishing family.

For a complete list of books and to
sign up for our newsletter,
go to DownAndOutBooks.com.

A Scholar of Pain
Grant Jerkins

ABC Group Documentation
an imprint of Down & Out Books
February 2018
978-1-946502-15-5

In his debut short fiction collection, Grant Jerkins remains—as the *Washington Post* put it—"Determined to peer into the darkness and tell us exactly what he sees." Here, the depth of that darkness is on evident, oftentimes poetic, display. Read all sixteen of these deviant diversions. Peer into the darkness.

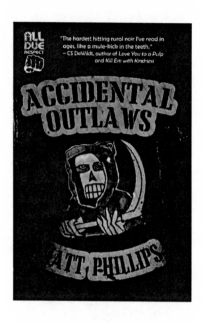

Accidental Outlaws
Matt Phillips

All Due Respect,
an imprint of Down & Out Books
December 2017
978-1-946502-44-5

Three linked crime novellas that follow working class antiheroes as they indulge in theft, murder, and lawless shenanigans. Ain't no cops running things out this way. In "Mesa Boys," Ronnie plots a haphazard heist with a twisted con man. In "The Feud," tough-as-nails Rex lets his resentment for a local pot dealer cloud his judgement. And, in "Bar Burning," a mysterious drifter goes toe-to-toe with his new lady's psychotic ex-husband.

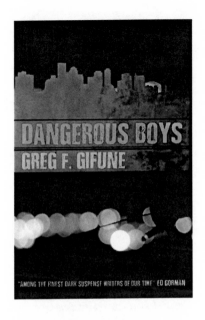

Dangerous Boys
Greg F. Gifune

Down & Out Books
March 2018
978-1-946502-52-0

All they had was each other…and nothing to lose…

Part coming-of-age tale, part dark crime thriller, *Dangerous Boys* is the story of a group of young punks with nothing left to lose, fighting to find themselves, their futures, and a way out of the madness and darkness before it's too late.

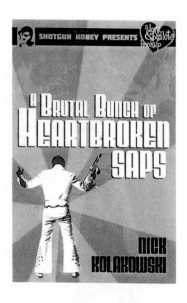

A Brutal Bunch of Heartbroken Saps
A Love & Bullets Hookup
Nick Kolakowski

Shotgun Honey, an imprint of
Down & Out Books
May 2017
978-1-943402-81-6

Bill is a hustler's hustler with a taste for the high life…who suddenly grows a conscience. However, living the clean life takes a whole lot of money, and so Bill decides to steal a fortune from his employer before skipping town.

Pursued by crooked cops, dimwitted bouncers, and a wise-cracking assassin, Bill will need to be a quick study in the way of the gun if he wants to survive his own getaway. Who knew that an honest attempt at redemption could rack up a body count like this?

CPSIA information can be obtained
at www.ICGtesting.com
Printed in the USA
LVOW12s0041090118
562346LV00001B/164/P